Praise for *The Age of*]

"Wild and oddly touching . . . Marcus has created a thought-provoking, completely singular work." —*Los Angeles Times*

"Don't walk into this world expecting to know which way is up; just sit back and enjoy the view from a completely new perspective." —*Details*

"A genuinely original book . . . *The Age of Wire and String* is a convincing . . . book in which states are translated into will-less objects. And while it may seem simply off-beat, it possesses the sort of closet-rationale one might expect from a follower of the French Oulipo movement or the so-called 'Martian' school of poets." —*The London Times*

"This book is a coolly lyrical, sometimes tongue-in-cheek, pseudo-scientific description of the Earth and the life of its various populations-as though Marcus were a sociologist describing the world in which everything is wired to everything else. . . . *The Age of Wire and String* anticipates a career devoted to intelligent exploration of major themes."
—Kelly Cherry, *Chicago Tribune*

"A rare, genius-struck achievement . . . filled with great beauties, high themes, enormous sorrows." —*Kirkus Reviews*

"Utterly wonderful, wonderful and beautiful. A world appears made of birds, dogs, odd bits of the Self, and ancient impressions of the very first things—Father and Mother, strange foods, a storm in the sky outside-all the elements of ordinary life systematically recombined to give substance to feeling and sensation, our deepest and most hidden knowledge of home." —Donald Antrim

"In his entirely self-generated possible world, Ben Marcus immolates American notions about family, culture, and the domestic drama, and asks questions later. What remains in the epicenter of the conflagration are fragile, longing, and funny ruminations on the secret lives of objects and environments-written in some of the most breathtaking prose I've encountered lately." —Rick Moody

"This doesn't happen very often. Somebody comes out of left field and blows up literature. In the authoritative tone of the product manual, Ben Marcus describes the operation of an impossible world that, page by page, becomes increasingly plausible and affecting. With the danger of using the degraded language to which this book is the antidote, I'd say *The Age of Wire and String* marks the debut of a highly intelligent and exacting literary mind." —Jeffrey Eugenides

"Ben Marcus's first book is a stream of pure oxygen. Delicately sustained and varied linguistic displacements rigorously reinvent our society and provide it with a mythology both ancestral and brand-new. This new world is as baffling as the one we've been taking for granted, and magically compelling. If you want to find out what you should really think, this is the book you should read." —Harry Mathews

"A combination of gorgeous, sensuous realism and disjointed action, Marcus's clear eye for the suburban sublime allows his definitions—of the structures and categories we impose on our-selves, of the people in his life and of hidden 'natural' phenomena—to resonate in a way that is much richer than, say, Douglas Coupland's inventories of pop culture . . . This debut collection may just succeed in sneaking prose-poetry to a wider, younger audience." —*Publishers Weekly*

"All-embracing in its short-circuiting of pop culture, *The Age of Wire and String* is indisputably a work of genius. It makes postmodernism look like the work of preschoolers." —Brian Evenson, *Grid*

"Ben Marcus must be thanked whole-heartedly for this breath of fresh air." —Marc Chfenetier, *American Book Review*

"Ben Marcus sets about to renew vision and reinstate mystery . . . A uniquely extraordinary book which is, along with all its delights, a brilliant telling of the human tragedy." —Rikki Ducornet, *Rain Taxi*

"In sculpting his mysterious pastiches, Marcus employs both restraint and heavily connotative vocabulary; so while the narrative is often deliberately wooden, a sensation of lack and pathos also lurk, the sort of haunting tenderness that is often linked with memory."
—Stacey Levine, *The Stranger*

"It's surreal, but not dada; fantastic, but not fantasy or sf; mysterious, but not a mystery; fiction, but almost totally lacking in characters, plot or drama . . . This highly original work will appeal to ambitious readers who enjoy Joyce, Beckett, or other writers who confound our assumptions about language and perception. A potential cult classic."

—*Library Journal*

"Marcus has written a primer for a new way of looking at the commonplace . . . [His] intriguing experimentation is vital to the growth of the language and letters. Marcus blazes a trail to a new place in literature. Whether one wants to follow depends on the reader's sense of adventure."

—*Tulsa World*

"Here are stories so brilliant, so amazingly fresh, yet so strange . . . that most readers will be left speechless, bewildered or angry (or all three) . . . A wild flight of imagination . . . [Marcus] crafts a sentence or constructs a vignette that is pure gold, proving that his stories are held together by more than baling wire and chewing gum."

—Lee Milazzo, *Dallas Morning News*

"It's a cross between a scientific manual, *Monty Python* and a kind of Bible, with a surreal and opaque logic of its own . . . Full of weird non sequiturs and a kind of Lewis Carroll nonsense, with words and themes colliding in ways that are frequently touching and funny."

—*The Observer* (London)

"I believe this book has a place within the chaotic tradition of Sterne's *Tristram Shandy*." —*The Telegraph* (London)

"Wondrous and slyly witty . . . *The Age of Wire and String* will find its fans among those people who relish prose that mimics dream, who love it when words are used as they once were, and incantations, as spells."

—*The Idler*

BOOKS BY BEN MARCUS

The Age of Wire and String
Notable American Women
Leaving the Sea
The Flame Alphabet
The Father Costume (with Matthew Ritchie)
The Anchor Book of New American Short Stories, ed.
New American Stories, ed.
Notes from the Fog

THE AGE OF WIRE AND STRING

stories by Ben Marcus

DALKEY ARCHIVE PRESS

DALLAS, TX / ROCHESTER, NY

First Dalkey Archive edition, 1998
Second printing, 2004
Third printing, 2007
Fourth printing, 2024

Library of Congress Cataloging-in-Publication Data:
Marcus, Ben, 1967-
The age of wire and string : stories / Ben Marcus. — 1st Dalkey Archive ed.
p.   cm.
ISBN 1-56478-196-8 (pb : alk. paper)
I. Title.
[PS3563.A6375A7 1998b]
813'.54—dc21 98-23361
CIP

Grateful acknowledgement is made to the editors of the publications in which
portions of this book first appeared: *After Yesterday's Crash, Conjunctions, Grand
Street, The Iowa Review, Pushcart Prize XX, The Quarterly, StoryQuarterly,* and
Yearbook.

for Father

CONTENTS

Every word was once an animal.

—EMERSON

Mathematics is the supreme nostalgia of our time.
—MICHAEL MARCUS

ARGUMENT

THIS BOOK IS a catalog of the life project as prosecuted in the Age of Wire and String and beyond, into the arrangements of states, sites, and cities and, further, within the small houses that have been granted erection or temporary placement on the perimeters of districts and river colonies. The settlement, in clusters and dispersed, has long required a document of secret motion and instruction—a collection of studies that might serve to clarify the terms obscured within every facet of the living program.

There is no larger task than that of cataloging a culture, particularly when that culture has remained willfully hidden to the routine in-gazing practiced by professional disclosers, who, after systematically looting our country of its secrets, are now busy shading every example of so-called local color into their own banal hues. A catalog of poses and motions produced from within a culture may read, then, like a form of special pleading, or, at the very least, like a product that must be ravaged of bias by scholars prepared to act as objective witnesses. It has, however, been demonstrated by Sernier (and others, although without violence) that the outer gaze alters the inner thing, that by looking at an object we destroy it with our desire, that for accurate vision to occur the thing must be trained to see itself, or otherwise perish in blindness, flawed.

It is under such terms that *The Age of Wire and String* sets forth to present an array of documents settling within the chief concerns of the society, of any society, of the world and its internal areas. To pretend that there are other concerns is to pretend. Let this rather be the first of many forays into the mysteries, as here disclosed but not destroyed. For it is in these things that we are most lost, as it is in these things alone that we must better be hidden.

SLEEP

Intercourse with Resuscitated Wife

INTERCOURSE WITH RESUSCITATED wife for particular number of days, superstitious act designed to insure safe operation of household machinery. Electricity mourns the absence of the energy form (wife) within the household's walls by stalling its flow to the outlets. As such, an improvised friction needs to take the place of electricity, to goad the natural currents back to their proper levels. This is achieved with the dead wife. She must be found, revived, and then penetrated until heat fills the room, until the toaster is shooting bread onto the floor, until she is smiling beneath you with black teeth and grabbing your bottom. Then the vacuum rides by and no one is pushing it, it is on full steam. Days flip past in chunks of fake light, and the intercourse is placed in the back of the mind. But it is always there, that moving into a static-ridden corpse that once spoke familiar messages in the morning when the sun was new.

Snoring, Accidental Speech

SNORING, LANGUAGE DISTURBANCE caused by accidental sleeping, in which a person speaks in compressed syllables and bulleted syntax, often stacking several words over one another in a distemporal deliverance of a sentence. The snoring person can be stuffed with cool air to slow the delivery of its language, but perspiration froths at key points on the hips and back when artificial air is introduced, and thus the sleep becomes sketchy and riddled with noise. It is often best to cull the sleeper forth from static communication by responding to its snores with apneic barks—sounds produced without air. The effect of the barks is to isolate each aspect of the snore sound by slowing down the delivery—riding the sleeper until the snore breaks into separate words. Decoders should sit on the bed and jostle the sleeper's stomach. This further dispatches the clusters that often form when the sleeper speaks all at once (snores). The decoder is then better able to decipher the word blocks. When analyzed, the messages are often simple. Pull me out, they say, the water has risen to the base of my neck.

Sky Destroys Dog

AIR DAYS IN the Western Worship Boxes, traditionally the Wednesday, Friday, and Half-Man Day following the first Sunday that a dog has suffocated the weather. They were days of foodless observance to sanctify the season of Charles, which was notable for its storms of airlessness and heavy frontals near the north that caused all but the dogs to retreat to the air hostels. Air days are of very ancient and uncertain origin. The dates of their celebration are now determined by dog descendants (similar to the Labrador, but with the additional storm lung) rather than by the universal storm calendar and are frequently called "days of air for food." Difficulties with dog populations in the Western Worship Boxes generated the mass suffocation of Ohio (1973), and the speed-fasting experiments of Buffalo and Schenectady (1980–1982), in which the Western population of those cities mistimed the exit day of their religious food-minus, thus breaking their fasts before the season of Charles had restored air to their homes, when the storm dogs still stalked the houses, breathing up the airless wind and eating the air and rain, praying to Charles that the people would not return.

Air Trance 16

IF THE MOTION of wind were to be slowed, as weather is slowed briefly when an animal is born, we would notice a man building and destroying his own house. If we speak to the man through a dense rain, our speech is menaced by the DROWNING METHOD, and we appear to him to be people that are angry and shouting. If my father is the man we are looking at, he will shout back at me, protecting the house with his hand, and his voice will blend with whatever weather he has decided to create in the sky between us to form a small, hard animal, which, once inside me, will take slow, measured, strategic bites. The animal's eating project will produce in others the impression that I am kneeling, lying, or fading in an area of total rain, taking shelter behind my upraised hand. Since they will be standing above me, the people will need to request special powers of vision, which will be immediately granted, in order that I appear in slow, original colors, viewed from any possible perspective, chewing with great care at my own body while the house gets smashed behind me.

The Death of Water

IT IS SOFT, malleable, ductile, iron-gray fluid with hexagonal or cubic ice structure. It is slightly harder than air. It is the most abundant of the RARE WATERS of group 111b of the water graph. It does not tarnish rapidly in dry grass but quickly loses its luster when swallowed. It oxidizes slowly in ALBERT and rapidly in LOUISE. It is attacked by solutions of RICHARD 3 and by concentrated or dilute SAMANTHA 7G. When heated, it burns with a brilliant flame to form a river that exhibits fishes and stones and is used in shuttling the seven primary, liquid emotions to the BEHAVIOR FARM. The steam is used as a core for the carbon arteries of OHIO. The element forms relationships with ancient water. An alloy of water is used as the flint in house films. Minute particles of this water ignite in the air when scratched from the surface of the larger mass. Its death is assembled by electrolysis of the drinking glass or by reduction of the fused canoe with sand. Death was realized in 1807 in the water as a new erosion by Carolina and by England and Thompson; it was named for the hills and swells in Deerborne, which had been killed only two years earlier. The nearly complete funeral was not produced until 1875, after which waterfalls and streams and bodies of further water began to gush down and dribble and then stop, as the sky's eulogy declined and graves on all sides began their fluid opening.

TERMS

LEG INITIATIONS   Act or technique of preparing the legs for sleep. They may be rubbed, shaved, or dressed in pooter.

ALBERT   Nightly killer of light, applied to systems or bodies which alter postures under various stages of darkness. Flattened versions exist only in the water or grass. They may not rise until light is poured upon them.

PROFESSIONAL SLEEPERS   Members whose sleep acts perform specific, useful functions in a society. Clustered sleepers ward off birds; single, submerged sleepers seal culprits in houses; dozers heaped in cloth enhance the grasses of a given area, restore belief in houses.

SADNESS   The first powder to be abided upon waking. It may reside in tools or garments and can be eradicated with more of itself, in which case the face results as a placid system coursing with water, heaving.

SLEEP HOLES   Areas or predesigned localities in which dormant figures and members conduct elaborate sleep performances. Points are scored for swimming, riding, and killing. Some members utilize these sites to perfect their sleep speech, in order to profess the dozer's knowledge. Others exercise or copulate or rapidly eat cloth and grain. The father slept in one for four hours while smashing his own house, which contained its own sleepers, who performed nothing.

BIRD SEVEN   1. Period in which members Linda through early Rachel engaged in storm pantomimes. 2. Year of the body. 3. Last moment in which the skin of a member gains oracular capacity of wind trapping. 4. The first day of life. 5. The end times.

SHIRT OF NOISE   Garment, fabric, or residue that absorbs and holds sound, storing messages for journeys. Its loudness cannot be soothed. It can destroy the member which inhabits it.

NITZEL'S GAMBLE   The act or technique of filling the lungs with water. The chance was first taken by the Nitzel in Green River.

SUN STICK   Item of the body which first turns toward sun when a member dies, sleeps, collapses. It is the pure compass toward tracts that are heated and safe, also called true places.

WIND BOWL   Pocket of curved, unsteady space formed between speaking persons. They may discuss the house, its grass, some foods, the father inside. The wind bowl will tilt and push across their faces, that they might appear leaning back, arching away from each other, grasping at the ground behind them as if sleeping.

SALT   An item that comprises the inner and outer core of most to all animals. An animal may be licked free of this salt, or an animal may be hosed clean or scraped. Only when it coughs up salt or otherwise produces salt matter from within can the animal be expected in a short time to collapse outward and exit the place of confinement.

SLEEPING GROUP   Team of members which performs mutual, radical sleep acts in various sites of varying difficulty. They are satisfied not with primary sleeping but with watching the sleeping of others. These are members which can copulate, speak, or eat only when surrounded by fields of tossing sleepers that are weeping, are moaning, are struggling to breathe.

JENNIFER   The inability to see. Partial blindness in regard to hands. To jennifer is to feign blindness. The diseases resulting from these acts are called jennies.

$$\overline{\text{GOD}}$$

Bird to the North, Act of Wind

GOD RIDES BIRD to the north, act of wind implemented against the stationary position of most oceans. Certain weather is not recognized by the land it is practiced on; funnel clouds necessarily unravel or bank off any crusted terrain, hailstones and other atmospheric shale burn into water before the city receives them, whole temperate zones dissipate over a lake and suck upward. The act of riding procures a medical wind to heal these stagnations. The lark, the griffin, and the mallard, all birds of indeterminate temperature and vapor content, function as ignitors of the tide. For a ripple to spool downwind unobstructed, it must be set into force by the proper god riding above, often laced into the fur of a low-flying bird. What happens here is the beating of air into a still surface, the jostle-weave of the bird twisting off the new waves, and the swoop of the weather behind it as the plumage of the carrier ignites and recedes off the god-channeler's hands, dispatched with a blessing to unfurl and storm above the new-moving ocean.

Died

PARKER, MARK, A body king fighting the darkness person Albert, which nightly killed the persons of light; with his sun stick, he also killed the person's home; after killing the entire person, he was attacked by a winter Albert (possessing underground extremities [sublimbs]), which he killed with another stick (Nagle), but died himself, accompanied by Mary (keening), and in agony seeing the new persons that were walking freely, unnamed, beyond the reach of the sun.

G–D

IT IS A mode entered by flaxen tree tools from three to twelve lawns long, sometimes curved slightly, with conical bore and a cup-shaped godpiece. It produces only the natural angels of the city, slightly modified, however, by the materials of the landbound heaven. North of its leaves, the tool is used to call wasps into the bore to shape the angels as they are wept against the grass.

Warning: It is what often clogs the port. It is heavily sugared. It channels mouth steam (frusc) into the back bunt of the willow. Here is where angels amass in surplus and cease to breathe. The wings grow sticky and no longer beat.

Only the lawns feeding upward afford the angels an exit once the bore is lost: Needle grass pierces the tool at the hind; sugar clouds the bore, tilting the wasps from the saddle graft; and the godpiece contracts slightly at the cup, popping angels through the holes in succession until the willow tool can once again lift from the lawn into the skylike areas, to proceed in dragging its crying onto other grassland territories.

Landing on Floating Island of the Gods

LANDING ON FLOATING island of the gods without invitation, form of deafness exemplified by reckless flying. The flier is within the wind, is an aspect of human weather. When one of the senses is stalled, a form of deviant weather occurs where the wind's bits (fliers) do not adhere to the arc of their origin. This causes all kinds of crazy landings. The particular deafness spoken of here effects breaches formerly unheard of; the flier will glide unknowingly past the warnings of others, he will focus only on a lush strip of green-and-gold earth seemingly floating in the middle skin of the atmosphere. The gods are there. With closed eyes, they are flying tiny birds over a fire. Then from the sky a man hurtles downward, the sound of the gods washing past him like colored wind, his fingers twisting in elaborate shapes of speech. The gods turn their heads into the smell of the roasting food, their dream erased by a dark rupture in the sky.

Ethics of Listening When Visiting
Areas That Contain Him

THE CONFESSION OF father is instituted by a low, glass-covered frame structure for starting speeches. It differs from a LISTENING FRAME only in that the soil is heated by day—either artificially by underground electric wiring or graveyard pipes, or naturally with women's manure. The manure is first folded daily until the initial period of strong fermentation is over; it is then mixed with a garment of the father, placed in the bottom of the receptacle, and covered with an appropriate amount of soil. Heat is produced by the union of the waste and the rag. Visitations occur by one family member. Note: If the child goes to the garden to absolve him, he should bring a burlap bag. This reduces the necessity of covering the grave with blankets or other insulation at night, when the one underground is shivering too much to speak.

TERMS

CLOUD SHIMS   Trees, brush, shrubs, or wooden planks that form the walls of the heaven container. These items are painted with blues and grays and the golds of the earliest sky. They are tiny, although some are large. They exist mainly to accommodate the engravings of the container, allowing a writable surface to exist aloft. The engravings command the member down or up, in or out, or back, back and away from here.

CROONAL   A song containing information about a lost, loved, or dead member. These are leg songs or simple wind arrangements. They are performed by the Morgan girl, who has run or walked a great distance and cannot breathe. She fashions noises between her hands by clapping and pumping her homemade air.

TREASURE OF POSSIBLE ENUNCIATIONS   Catalog of first, last, and intermediate lexia. It includes all possible words and their unutterable opposites. Other than Thompson's Bank of Communicable Desire, no other such comprehensive system exists.

GOD CHARGE   Amount or degree of Thompson occurring in a person or shelter.

HEEN VIEWING   1. The act, technique, or practice of viewing, with intent to destroy, any object or residue within or upon the house. Punishments of such acts include demotion to lower house, in which the culprit is subjected to endless attentions, proddings, mountings, and group viewings by an unbroken stream of voluntary wardens. 2. To covet the life of another. 3. To look at a body and wish to destroy it. The heen in this case occurs or emanates from the hips, and the term applies in all cases less the one in which a member is looking upon, and wishing to terminate, his own body, which act goes unpunished.

HEAVEN   Area of final containment. It is modeled after the first house. It may be hooked and slid and shifted. The bottom may be sawed through. Members inside stare outward and sometimes reach.

FIEND, THE   1. Heated thing. 2. Item or member which burrows under the soil. 3. Item which is eaten postday. 4. Any aspect of Thompson which Thompson cannot control.

GOD-BURNING SYSTEM   Method of Thompsonian self-immolation. For each Thompson, there exist flammable outcrops or limbs which rub onto the larger body of Thompson (Perkins), rendering morning fires and emberage that lights the sky and advances the time of a given society or culture.

GODPIECE   Cup, bowl, or hoop, which, when swished through air, passed under water, or buried for an indefinite time in sand will attract fragments and other unknown grains that comprise the monetary units of a given culture. The godpiece is known further as a wallet, satchel, or bag that assigns value to the objects inside it.

HEAVEN CONSTRUCTION THEORY   The notion brought to bear on the construction of the final shelter. All work in this area is done under the influence of the first powder, so the hands may shake, the eyes be glazed, the body be soft and movable.

LIVING, THE   Those members, persons, and items that still appear to engage their hands into what is hot, what is rubbery, what cannot be seen or lifted.

MATH GUN, THE   1. Mouth of the father, equipped with a red freckle, glistening. It is shined by foods, dulled with water, left alone by all else. 2. His pencil. It shortens with use and must be shaved, trimmed, or sharpened by the person, who follows behind with a knife.

PERKINS   1. Term given to the body of Thompson, in order that His physical form never desecrate His own name. 2. The god of territory.

RAG, THE, OR PRAYER, RAG   Device of stripped or pounded cloth, held to the mouth during prayer.

STRING THEORY OF FATIGUE   System or technique of diagnosing the level of exhaustion in a member by covering it with medical ropes.

RARE WATERS, THE   Series of liquids containing samples of the first water. It is the only water not yet killed. It rims the eyes, falls from them during certain times, and collects at the feet, averting the grasp of hands, which are dry, and need it.

SUN STALLS   Abrupt disruptions in the emissions of the sun. They occur in the blazing quarter strips which flap. There begins a clicking or slow sucking sound. Members standing below arch or bend. They raise a hand to the ear or eye, form a cup or shield.

WEATHER BIRTHING   1. The act or technique of selecting and reciting certain words within given, fixed sky situations with the intent of generating, enhancing, or subtracting weather from a given area in the society. 2. Burning the skin of a member to alter the sky shapes of a locality. 3. Placing powders or other grains in the mouth while speaking to alter the temperature of a local site. 4. Whispering while holding birds in the mouth.

BEEF SEEDS   Items, scraps, or buttons that bear forth fibrous tissue striata after being buried under milk-loaded cloth.

WESTERN WORSHIP BOXES   The smallest structures, designed to fit precisely one body. They are rough-walled and dank, wooden and finely trimmed—the only areas of devotion. When more than one body enters to worship as a team, the box gevorts.

NAGLE   Wooden fixture which first subdued the winter Albert. It occurs in and around trees and is highly brown.

LEGAL PRAYER   Any prayer, chant, or psalm affixed with the following rider:

> Let a justifiable message be herewith registered in regard to desires and thoughts appertaining to what will be unnamed divinities, be they bird forms or other atmo bestial manifestations of the CONTROLLING THOMPSON, or instead unseen and personless concoctions of local clans, groups, or teams. With no attempt to imprint here a definitive lingual string of terms that shall be said to be terms bearing a truthful and antidisharmonic concordance to the controlling agent, witnesses may accord to themselves the knowledge that a PRAYER is being committed that will herewith be one free of flaws, snags, and lies. It will not be a misdirected, unheard, or forgotten prayer. Neither will the blessed recipient be possessed of any confusion with respect to who or what has offered this prayer for consideration, although this assertion shall not indicate that the powerless subject makes any claim of authority over the DIVINE AGENT OF FIRE. It shall be a direct and honest gesturation to be received by said agent and dispatched

or discarded in a custom that the agent knows. This now being said in the manner of greatest force and fluid legal acuity, the prayer can begin its middle without fear of repercussive sky reversals or blows that might destroy the mouth of the humble subject on his knees.

FOOD

The Food Costumes of Montana

IN THE MORNING in Montana the leg was bound from the ankle to the knee with bacon or hair and then cross-gartered with thongs or strips of uncut rice; later a slack taffy, bound at the ankle, was worn. As the lower legs of the taffy became more fitted, they were called slews, and as the slews eroded or spoiled to the knee, fitted milk skins called loops were worn. By 11:30 a.m., feet were added to the loops. As slews grew shorter, loops became longer; by c. 12:20 p.m., the loops reached the hips and were attached by butter webs to the stomach. By c. 1:00, the loops and slews formed one garment; thus shads were first known. Beans and nuts were used, as was kale, and color became extravagant. The shads were multicolored and often each leg was clothed in a contrasting food style. As the upper part of the loops became more decorated and puffed out, a separation occurred (c. 2:30); the upper part became known as pike rings because of the swimming motion the food made as it circled the thigh, and the leg coverings were for the first time called bones and recognized as a separate accessory of dress. Knitted bones were first known in Oklahoma (3:27); in Montana, Linder is said to have worn (c. 4:00) the first knitted vegetable bones for a record-setting period of three minutes before succumbing. Knitting thereafter became general, and machines came into use after autumn of that hour. Colored, cooked, and reversed pike rings were worn at 5:15, though cooled wheat sleeves were the fashion. Also at that hour the decorative bean boots of the army were of the northern or navy style, although oaten socks were shared by sisters during the 5:30 festival. Cereals came into use after 6:00. Noodles, because of their strength and elasticity, became the leading loop fiber after the Evening War. At 7:30, women began applying the fudge girdle, a one-piece garment that spread from waist to feet. As men's milk slews spoiled throughout the evening, their loops grew shorter and fresher, and the word *food* officially came into use just after sunset. Women's food, although hidden until midnight by their skirts, has always been an important part of their costume. It is expected to remain fresh for many days, and will certainly survive the women who wear it and the men who look at it.

First Green

THE CLAIM THAT he has destroyed the garden is no more than
a stunt of those who would replant it from their prison cells. Such
flowers and shrubs as were exterminated by man had long been
leading a separate existence, whose last hideouts the warden swept
away. Anyone who did not mourn the primary herbal loss was forced
into inner emigration years before the first seeds were delivered
from the sky: At the latest, with the stabilization of the American
flower bed, coinciding with wild grasses and their smoldering, garden
culture corrected itself in the spirit of the midland illustrated prison
books, which yielded little to that of the freed man's edict of the
fossilized forest, desert-grass roadways, and pretentious tulip gods
built over homes and churches to honor what was initially seen as
a generous sky. The whole span of the garden was languishing for
its man, and it is an injustice to the editors of *House-Lock Press* or
to the reorganizers of the captured flower series to reproach them
with timeserving under the man gardener. They were always like
that, and their line of least resistance to the printed seeds they manufactured was continued undeflected in the line of least resistance
to a Man Regime, among whose seed theories, as the warden
himself declared, freed-man seed patterns in the sky ranked highest.
This has led to a fatal toxicity. Bulbs dropped from jailbox windows

practiced a form of the new air blooming, new only because sacrifices had cleansed the sky of pollen, creating a fertility of air that matched easily that of the richest soils. For the prison to reside fully within the flower, the appropriate gods were said to demand a full, floral patterning: Any garden struck to live in widths of sky (and so confine a collection of men) must project a man pattern upward. The air tattoos warned only those men who had until then avoided incarceration by unearthing any and all sprigs of the seed of god. What was called destruction by the prisoners was instead a clever exile practiced by those few who remained alive beneath the gardens. Any attempt to recapture even the smallest aspect of sky required a poisoning of roots, which action they achieved by breathing in combined efforts beneath the heaviest stalks. When some shrubs did erode, revealing skies printed with man shapes to those living below the gelatinous prison buffers, actual prison masonry became incorporated into flower movements as the garden fought to survive the poisoning. These stone shrubs drooped beneath the prison scaffolding. Those who were still called men could do nothing but decorate this new stone ceiling, using, of course, the colored air rendered from their combined breathing to stain the rocks with images of themselves and what little else they knew. But the distortion of these facts to support a prison publishing industry whose main concern is a revision of the first planting is little less savage than smashing one's grandfather in the face for embellishing slightly his story of the river town in the which he was raised. No amount of book-style illusion will alter the origin of plants. Nor will man-shrubs bidden airwise to honor what are now less than men affect in any way the flower scheme as it is destined to be practiced by the one honest god remaining.

Brian, Treated to a Delicate Meal

BRIAN, TREATED TO a delicate meal, a method of keeping travelers at bay. Most instances of travel will offer several opportunities for sleeping within a short time; the rising traveler will encounter the sleeping or eating traveler during this period. Denying Brian food can be used to encourage the travelers to sleep, or to remain lying down until Brian is fed. The energy of travelers is supplied vertically, through the feet; therefore, the sleeping traveler is temporarily cut off from this supply, and Brian remains hungry. Locomotion installs sleepiness, and a field, called a somnalian area, is generated in the doorway of the dining car. The dichotomy between the sleeping and nonsleeping traveler extends beyond states of alertness. When the traveler is vertical, he will be resisted by the somnalian field in front of the dining car because of his high content of energy, and a positive charge will be issued within the dining room, enabling a delicate meal to be served to Brian. This field is, in part, generated by the horizontal (sleeping or nonsleeping) traveler, who, because of his low or nonexistent energy, is the only traveler able to eat. For the sake of keeping Brian fed, some travelers are kept sleeping at all times. A traveler who resists sleeping but remains horizontal for three passes through this cycle will briefly ascend the chain, and pass a rising traveler and go on to eat.

Food Storms of the Original Brother

THE BROTHER IS built from food, in the manner of minute particles slowly settling or suspended by slight currents, that exist in varying amounts in all air. There is least food-printing over the ocean and most at low levels over cities; food caused by airplanes is a serious addition to a radical new man-making practiced in versions of Detroit, and explains at least partially the heavy food-fall there. Sources of atmospheric food that can be utilized in the assembling and fall of men are:

1. Winds blowing skin from birds (the skin is a wrap-bag for grains).
2. The various products of combustion at festivals (the brother process in the seasonal Americas requires sufficient picnic heat or flak from any food fires).
3. Mountain breaks releasing flukes of grain (air matches fractures in the mountain and attracts food winds to seal the terrain).
4. Salt spray from the oceans (the strongest glue of food forms is salt in its glacial stage).
5. Bread and other material from plants (as ever, plant breads and their accompanying food posse allow the body to feed

upon itself in times of famine).

6. Bits of rain containing beef seeds (rains of the Americas derive from the cattle colonies of the South, often stealing beef from the livestock to thicken the water coverage of storms).

Food sometimes settles quickly on surfaces to precipitate the arrival of persons, but vast assembled dinners are delivered to the layered uppers of the air and suspended there until clouds of wheat and beans breed forth men parts to bond in the salt rinds of lowest air. The effects of an eruption of tree bread such as that in Larchmont have been observed three years after its occurrence. Anthroscopic food particles (those to which men adhere) are the nuclei of man-making in free air; the nucleus of each head in a fogbank or cloud and of armseeds in each rainball and snowshard is one of these invisible particles of first foods. Jason Marcus, the original brother, who in 1990 invented a device for counting the air, first correlated food particles and persons. The food that he discovered comprising his person is also chiefly responsible, through its scattering effect upon light (sun stalls), for one type of darkness that is observed when he takes his falls through and above the land, eating and rebuilding parts of himself in a small cyclone of black seeds and grains.

Hidden Food, from Above

THE CHIEF LEGAL problem connected with hidden food is that of title. A scavenger cannot acquire title to chicken that he has discovered abruptly, and therefore he cannot transfer title even by barter to an innocent dining man who has requested a stew. Hence the rightful owner of the chicken may take it without compensation from anyone who has not properly tracked it according to the rules set forth by the *Topographical Legend and Location of Food Nooks*. The innocent dining man, however, may challenge the scavenger for breach of his implied warranty of good title as it applies to edible objects, in this case the promised delivery of a chicken bisque with definite ownership. These rules invariably apply to food hidden within houses, churches, and other recognizable structures; in certain townships, they obtain also when potatoes and bread are camouflaged within a manufactured landscape. Artificial food (Carl) is often used to disguise the presence of real food in these settings. The law respecting the transfer of dough and sugar suspended from the hips of a citizen differs somewhat. There, if the scavenger has authentically scented the pastry using the traditional methods of tracking (the crab walk, odor spiraling, or simple persistence with the food map of Yvonne), he takes an absolute title. To be such a purchaser, he must pay for the sweetened dough with something of value (usually a loaf of sugar-soaked grain or a spore wand from the food spring of the Kenneth sisters) and must not be aware of anything suspicious concerning the citizen on whom the confections have been hidden. The person from whom the dough was initially procured may recover it (paying with a pound of custard) from a holder who is not a bona fide scavenger, but, rather, a passive recipient of food that has not been concealed. Such a holder—e.g. one who received flugals or eclairs as a gift, or else reconstructed crumpets from the throat wall of a sleeping scavenger—is within his rights to criticize openly the prior endorsers of the pastries (residents who presented the snacks as "objects that were carefully hidden and then discovered") for breaching their implied warranty of good title, unless the endorsers had protected themselves in writing, carving the word "Mine" into the husk of the food treats in question.

TERMS

BLAIN   Cloth chewed to frequent raggedness by a boy. Lethal to birds. When blanketed over the house, the sky will be swept of objects.

CARL   Name applied to food built from textiles, sticks, and rags. Implements used to aid ingestion are termed, respectively, the *lens*, the *dial*, the *knob*.

CHOKE POWDER   Rocks and granules derived from the neck or shoulder of a member. If the mouth harness is tightened, the powder is issued in the saliva and comes to rim the teeth or coat the thong. For each member of a society, there exists a vial of powder. It is the pure form of this member, to be saved first. When the member is collapsing or rescinding, the powder may be retrieved by gripping the member's neck tightly and driving the knee into its throat.

EATING   1. Activity of archaic devotion in which objects such as the father's garment are placed inside the body and worshiped. 2. The act or technique of rescuing items from under the light and placing them within. Once inside the cavity, the item is permanently inscribed with the resolutions of that body and can therefore be considered an ally of the person. 3. Dying. Since the first act of the body is to produce its own demise, eating can be considered an acceleration of this process. Morsels and small golden breads enter the mouth from without to enhance the motions and stillnesses, boost the tones and silences. These are items which bring forth instructions from the larger society to the place of darkness and unknowing: the sticky core, the area within, the bone. 4. Chewing or imbibing elements that have escaped from the member or person into various arenas and fields.

CLOTH-EATERS, THE First group actively to chew, consume, and otherwise quaff extensive bolts and stacks of cloth.

TREE BREAD The victuals in concert with tree systems.

FOOD SPRING 1. The third season of food. It occurs after hardening, delivering a vital sheen to the product, which becomes juicy, colorful, light. It lasts for a period of moments, after which the edible begins to brown, sink, fade. 2. Vernal orifice through which foods emerge or cease to be seen.

FOOD MAP OF YVONNE, THE 1. Parchment upon which can be found the location of certain specialized feminine edibles. 2. Locations within a settlement in which food has been ingested, produced, or discussed. 3. Scroll of third Yvonne, comprised of fastened grain and skins. This document sustained the Yvonne when it was restricted from the home grave.

FOOD POSSE Group which eradicates food products through burial and propulsion. They cast, sling, heave, toss, and throw food into various difficult localities. Food that has been honored or worshiped is smothered with sand. Edibles shined, polished, or golded are rusted with deadwater. Snacks from the home are placed in the buttocks and crushed.

FUDGE GIRDLE, THE Crumpets of cooked or flattened chocolage, bound or fastened by wire. This garment is spreadable. It is tailored strictly with heat and string and is cooked onto the body of the ancient member. At fights and thrashings, the fiend is consumed through this girdle.

MOUTH HARDNESS, THE   1. Device for trapping and containing the head. Mouths are often stuffed with *items*—the only objects legally defined as suspicious or worthy of silent paranoid regard. A claim is therefore made that we eat suspicion and become filled with it. The harness is designed to block all ingestion. Gervin states: "His mouth will be covered with a wire web. He shall never eat. Nor may he ever take what is outside and bring it inside. His stomach will forever devise upon what is within." 2. A system applied to the head to prevent destruction or collapse while reading or absorbing code.

GERVIN   Deviser of first fire forms and larger heat emblems. The Gervin exists in person form in all texts but is strictly a symbol or shape in the actual society. To gervin is to accommodate heated objects against one's body. One may also gervin by mouthing heated items of one's own body: the hand, the eye, the cupped rim of the lips.

KENNETH SISTERS, THE   Devisers of first food spring—blond-haired, slim-hipped, large, working hands. They dug the base for what would later become Illinois. They lived to be, respectively, fifty-seven, seventy-one, nine, forty-five, eighteen, and forty.

STINKPOINT   Moment of odor slightly frontward from the producing body. Since all odors issue first into a fraction of the forward air, allowing them to fall into a member advancing in time, any member achieving or arriving in a stinkpoint is also said to be a creator and coconspirator of any smells and smell systems in the society.

SHADOW CELLS   The visible, viscous grain deposited upon any area recently blanketed in shadow. The cells may be packed into dough, then spread onto the legs or hips. They may darken or obscure the head for an infinite period.

SPEED-FASTING EXPERIMENTS   Activity or practice of accelerated food abstention. It was first conducted in Buffalo. The record death by fasting occurred in two days, through motor-starving and exhaustion, verbal.

STORM LUNG   Object which can be swallowed to forestall the effects of weather upon a body.

TOPOGRAPHICAL LEGEND AND LOCATION OF FOOD NOOKS   System of overmaps depicting buried food quadrants, sauce grooves, and faults or fissures in which grains and beans are caught. The cloth form of the map can be applied to the bodies of animals, to clarify areas in which hollows might have amassed.

ODOR SPIRALING   Tossing, turning, and flinging of the head so as to render radical, unknown odors in a locality.

THE HOUSE

The Golden Monica

THERE EXISTS IN some precincts the phenomenon of the intruder
or mad invader, who enters the American house in order to extinguish himself in the presence of the mister, the female, the children,
whomever. The man powers in, arranges a prison of wire or rope
onto the members of the shelter, and settles onto a comfortable
area—the rug, a layered blanket, the soft membrane of the floor—
to attain a posture of attention to his own body that will render its
demise. They are forced to watch, the family. He lights a fire, this
man. Or he arranges the appliances to emit the sensations of music,
acquits himself of the gentleman's dance in the center of the room,
queries the animal likeness carved into his garment. In other
versions he strips to his skin and manifests a final saying to his audience. Make no mistake, they are bound such with the wire or rope
that they are forced to acquire the status of audience to this act,
and then further to the self-created corpse, which singularly occu-
pies their attention until rescue arrives. The condition of corpse
is achieved with a lotion, usually. The intruder might apply a final
wound onto himself with pistol or kerm. This knife is curved, fluent
in the obstacles of bone and cloth.

What is interesting, as always, is the aftermath. The body, as
such, lies often coiled on the floor. Whosoever sits bound at the

perimeter must witness its stillness. The television, when activated, accompanies the temperature of the room with a purling forth of warm air, casting the captives under the bluish gild of the broadcast runnel. Thereafter, through unspecified elaborate means, a single figure from the bound hostages—and plural it is, always—manages to delimit himself from his lashed state and escape the site. It is this figure—the escapee who abandons his bound gang for some place of lesser tension—who not only is accused of a murder but confesses to one, thus absorbing the suicide as his own act, despite the weirdly meek pleas of his family, whose claims for his innocence sound hollow, fictional.

The acts of doing and watching are interchangeable here. It is the genius of the perpetrator of the monica to shift volition onto his audience. The spectacle is arranged to emanate from whoever watches it, where seeing is the first form of doing. The audience is deceived into a sense of creation for the act it has witnessed. A member of the family seems riotously certain that he has murdered through the body, attaining the kill.

The act is called a monica because a suicide is forced into the purview of an audience of hostages. It is an apt model for the assessment of the shelter and its forms, assembled in these locations under the rubric of the glimmering, new suicide—houses in which to die. The American areas, in constituency, collaborate to intrude and invade, looting the body of what it does not require, fortifying it with the American medicine of the final home. While any critical neologism made here will be shucked by the world's refusal to bear the statements of anyone but its author, a certain new assault can be claimed for a shelter that would close the body down, deny it light. This body will no longer heal itself, feign wellness, posture some possession of any type of solution. Indeed, where air or light does not exist, it will fashion its own, at whatever cost, whatever pain, extracting that tonic from its own ravaged materials. The witness to this body, and even (or especially) the figure who seeks to escape the welter of the home proposing the monica, will be transfixed at once by the style of death that each man achieves, rightly paralyzed in the beauty of a new mode of exit. And then ultimately, always, by necessity, he will feel certain that he has caused this disappearance, through some stillness or silence of his own.

It is simple, really. Where a house is, this man will maul it with noise and steam, scouring what is stuck and stubborn therein with a lather of golden light, producing an exit of life that is marked by the inception of a shadow. And the shadow takes up residence inside the world. And the shadow is a scar that will not soon be put off.

The Enemy in House Culture

THE NAME IS given to members of a pre-early East American culture in the Southwest, predecessors of the original SLEEPING GROUP. Because of the cultural continuity from the SHELTER WITNESSES to the sleeping group, via the drowsers and their string theory of fatigue, they are jointly referred to by archaeologists as the Enemy culture. They are so called because of their extensive and alert practice of house burial; by covering the shelters with seeds and baking them with fossilized sun steam, the team averted fireproof enemies. One system of dating places their arrival in the area as early as the wakeful period of 1979. They seem to have been at first nomadic air hunters, using wooden fire techniques, sleep holes, and the math gun for food. They lived chiefly in grass with grass floors and learned to grow milk and squash, probably from southern neighbors in what was then Utah. As they developed a more extensive food system, they dug pits and lined them with milk for house storage and later carried finished houses to the river as an offering to Perkins, to secure sleep knowledge or possibly to prevent the numbed limb slumbers under Arkansas grass, brought on by exposure to houses built without grains or steam. At some time, perhaps 1983, they were succeeded in the area by the ancestors of the sleeping group, who probably absorbed many of them by creating exhaustion in the fields. Some houses may have been moved and may have contained the ancestors of other shelter tribes, others might have resisted sleep migration and collapsed. Archaeologists divide the time of this culture into the house maker and the house destroyer periods; in the latter period, participants turned increasingly to nonuseful and abstract houses, eventually constructing the penetrating gevorts box, of which one thousand wooden units were made during the Texas-Ohio sleep collaboration, 1987. Gevortsing has subsequently become known as any act, intention, or technique that uses negative house imagery during the dream experience as a device to instruct inhabitants to sleep-kill or otherwise destroy themselves, their walls, windows, doors, or roofs upon waking, until a chosen version of the culture has been sufficiently driven from their home.

Works from the War Between
Houses and Wind

The Strategy of Grass

SHE WAS THE first grass guard of American shelters. Augmented by a man, usually, the girl wielded her shade stick so that the sun might never collaborate with the grass in destroying the house. It was the third, early time that houses were under attack from outside forces. House-crushing schemes were previously observed to no avail; indeed, shacks were burned nightly by sun water bogged upon grass, fire chalk scratched out tents and sheds, and cabins of the period were lobbed in fire by green weeds until the girl took employment on American lawns. The technique of shade has since this time allowed houses to flourish, with the dog being designated as the first shade-chaser, or, more formally, the Person. Although not human, the person holds an innate need to save the house.

Shade has throughout known times warded off enemies, particularly those dispatched by the fiend, if the fiend is defined as any item of great or medium heat, extending from a wire. Although shade is formally gray in color, red-hued shades permeate the lawns of Denver, and a colorless, cooling shade has been observed in the seventeen primary locations of Illinois. While shade was first disproved by Jerkins in his FARM EXPERIMENTS (in which he claimed that shade was a black sun welt to be soothed or corrected with water and straw), it has currently gained favor in the communities due to the expert wielding of the sun-smashing girl. No sun is actually ever touched by this employee. The dramatic nomenclature indicates merely deft stick skills, an abundance of strength in the fingers, and an impervious posture toward heat. A shade sprayer by trade, her work involves de- and re-housing areas when the sun is brightest, dodging the topographical witness scheme. The dog stalks the rubbered cooling skins across the lawn or over sections of house, acting also as a shade dragger when the girl is at work beneath the house. Although shade is mistrusted by many occupants, and has rarely been selected as a primary weapon, it must not be overlooked as a key defense against objects that might burn in to take the house from the air, in secret agency with the wires of the hallowed sun.

Since grass preceded the house, and is considered to be a grain yet older than wood, it must be wondered whether the grass wars of the 1820s contributed to the brief minus of houses observed during this era. That no shelters were in view either indicates perhaps a correlation with the hiding time of those same days.

Lawn boys were numerous in Ohio in the early weeks of the first seventies. Boys and their counterparts, including those at the level of first apprentice, were dispatched across lawns to serve as wind poles during the street storms of this period, and the shorter, sturdier boys (maronies) were often the first to blow back into the houses. This explains the rugged ornamentation of certain shelters in the Middle West, most notably those houses of the tower period that contain chronicles and prayers etched into the tubes that spilled over from the dome or turret. The taller, skinnier boys could more successfully deflect, block, or stall the wind from the house, and they became better known as stanchers, although salaries were meager and they were forced to work in teams, sharing and regurgitating the same meal. During the chalkier street storms, however, the boys went entirely unfed and often starved upon the lawn, creating skin flags, or geysers of bone and cloth, which during more elastic storms could ripple back and snap windows from a house until glass spilled into the air, cutting down the insect streams. What was left of the employees was then smothered by this powdered glass and air blood that fell upon them, rendering a burial site at each house. Houses of the period were named after the boys that died protecting them. Boy piles on grass were richest after storms—this residue was called gersh—and planting was heaviest until this fertilizer was rifled by scavengers—often young girls and their animal sisters, who dragged the soil away in sacks and wagons for burial and sang the lamentations of the house for their brothers, dead on the grass from fighting the wind.

Air Dies Elsewhere

When air kills itself in remote regions, the debris settles here on the grass, sharpening the points. Men of the house may not walk on these areas, nor may they ever observe the grass without pain in the chest and belly. They exist as figures which are doubled over, in static repose against the house territory. When children sleep on these points of lawn, the funeral of air passes just above their heads in a crosswind with the body. Funerals generally are staged in pollinated wind frames, so that the air can shoot to the east off of the children's breath, dying elsewhere along the way, allowing fresh, living air to swoop in on the blast-back to attack the house. This funeral-chasing ability of children explains why they are allowed outside during the daytime and back in again the next day. The Mother cleans the child's mouth with her finger and is said to act as a transom for the warring agencies of wind. This is why she is placed in the window, wires bobbing from each hand, bowing forward against the glass.

Other forms of sleeping also calm the sky. Wealthy landowners hire professional sleepers to practice their fits on key areas of the grounds. The best sleepers stuff their pockets with grass and sleep standing up. Many amateur sleepers never wake up, or never fall asleep. If a professional wakes and discovers a protector still sleeping, or unable to sleep and making an attempt of it—in the shed, for example, downwind of the house—he is permitted to practice smashes upon this body. Freelancers take their dream seizures near the door, and storms are said to be held in abeyance. They are paid according to success. Much booty has been disbursed, but no one has ever succeeded in sleeping so deeply that the house is not smashed upon waking.

If men or parts of men in the house regions are ever studied, it will be their feet or their forelegs—whichever object is comprised of a knuckle buried under taut, dry, hairless skin. The primary bulletin of these times ensues between grass and the paw. When we kill men, we kill them because we are sad. SADNESS develops in and outside of the house, either just after entering or just after leaving. These are also the times of war, when we encounter men losing or gaining the house and we have the opportunity to act upon them. The feet of men, through a tradition established outside of the Schedule of Emotions, are soaked in Corey, a chemical produced in grass after air has mixed the shape of the house. Experts believe that our bodies grow heavier after being noticed, lighter when touched, and remain the same when left alone. This is further true of the wires that generate sadness through the chimney and other open areas.

Rule of Exit

When the sun's wires are measured, we discover the coordinates for a place or places that shall hereafter be known as perfect or final or miraculous. The house shall be built here using soft blocks of wood and certain solidified emotions, such as tungsten. By nightfall, the bird counter will collapse, and a new or beginning man must be placed at the road to resume the tally while the construction continues. His harness will be a great cloth fixture bound unto his head, to protect his mouth from the destroying conflicts, lest strong birds sweep in on the wires to knock back the homes. Every house prayer shall for all time ever read thusly:

> *Please let the wires not have been crooked or falsely dangling or stretched by the demon sun, let our measurements be exact and true, and bless our perfect place with abundant grasses. Cover us in shade so that we are hidden in your color. Hide us from birds and wires and the wind that sends them. Let smoke conceal us during the storm life, and give us strong walls. Let not any stray wind break us down and we will honor you. Bless us and a great shelter will be made for you in the new season. Help us thrive. We lie low here in the place that you have given us. Please remember that you have killed us and you can kill us and we wait and long in our deepest hearts to be killed only by you. Let this be our last and final house. Amen.*

Exporting the Inner Man

COUGHING, IN HUMANS, device for transporting people or goods from one level to another. The term is applied to the enclosed structures of the throat as well as the open platforms used to provide vertical transportation within cars and while lying in bed; it is also applied to devices consisting of a continuous belt or chain with attached buckets for handling bulk material. Simple throat hoists were used from ancient times, often retrieving people whose whereabouts had long been unknown. This retrieval can be halted or staggered if any of the human air ports are obstructed, causing limbs of the body to inflate or swell during coughing. This is called expanded house, and, in effect, increases the area a person has available to himself to hide in. For effective retrieval, the coughing must be focused on a specific limb and requires an exact, crouching posture of the cougher. Otherwise, the hiding person will vanish inside the boggy limb from one secret place to another, skillfully avoiding the suction of the cough and remaining undetected.

Views from the First House

IT IS UNDERSTOOD in terms of the phenomenon of combustion as seen in wood and brick; it is one of the basic tools in human culture. In ancient America and earlier, it was considered one of the four basic objects, a substance from which all things were composed. Its great importance to humans, the mystery of its powers, and its seeming largeness have made the house divine or sacred to many peoples. As a god, it is a characteristic feature of Messonism, in which, as with many house-worshiping religions, houses are considered the earthly model or emblem of the HEAVEN shelter, the essential difference being that occupants of a house are instructed always to LOOK IN (strup), to examine the contents within a house (Chakay) and derive instructions and strategies from these, whereas with the heaven container it is only possible to LOOK OUT; the area is one-way constructed with cloud shims and cannot be seen into. Occupants, if any, must train their attention outward (bog); they must never be seen watching themselves or looking at any other objects within the house (heen viewing, forbidden, punished by expulsion to lower house). The belief that houses are sacred is universal in science, and such beliefs have survived in some highly hidden cultures, including those that destroy houses for food and fuel, as well as nomadic cultures whose members derive spontaneous houses from water, cloth, and salt.

The most carefully preserved shelter cult in America was that of Perkins, the first god of territory. His disciples forbade sleeping near, in, or on their houses because it was believed that the sleeper was the first to be attacked by the fiend. The fiend sailed off the south shadow of his own shelter, tacking in the wind bowl at the back door, while the slipstream that poured from his roof broke open the houses of Perkins and sealed any sleepers in a fossil of hot wind and crumbs. These became the crumbs of the fiend; the ones that were not eaten were used to rudder the house that the fiend rode. An implicit goal of the Perkins group was to douse this neck-laced chain of fossilized sleepers with salt as it keeled behind the house, in the hope that the sleepers might bloat into anchors and cancel the advance of the fiend.

A further American truth is that of John, a house/garment cor-relationist who developed the first shirt shelters and land scarves that were sufficiently large enough to supply a family with shelter while still outfitting them in rashproof garments that did not crush under. It was John's theory that a family member should exist within the confines of a garment hovel; naked collisions were notable in this interior, and sleeve rooms were often damp and difficult to traverse, but tailoring of such a shelter was achieved easily by zip-ping cloth onto a room or snapping hoods onto windows or dog doors. John claimed that when visitors traveled from one house to another, they entered a public garment area (the tunic) weaved of municipal cotton, in which garments were shared with other travelers until a house was reached. At this point, private house law dictated that the visitor permit body scrubbings, the application of skin pooter, shrinkage testing, and synchronized family walking train-ing before the resident family deemed the visitor worthy of sharing their clothing inside the larger house costume.

The ramifications of the human ideas about houses are tremendously complex and can never be exhausted, extending as they do into the concepts of heaven construction theory, which posits heaven as the only usable, cooled shelter from which one can safely witness or bog the endless combustion of god (self-banished house member), who by definition resides outside of the heaven house in a broken house of air, with no means of entering in again. There just remains the torching of this exile out on the lawn (sky), the swarming embers that pull down the trees (clouds), and the sparks that blacken the gravel and burn their way down through house after house after house (instruction from sun*).

---

*Never shall sun be allowed to approximate an entry into the house. The windows shall be blacked up with wind and no chimney shall exist, nor may vents be punched into the walls. If the door is necessary, a bag shall seal the frame. Heat will come, as always, from the inside.

TERMS

OHIO   The house, be it built or crushed. It is a wooden composition affixed with stones and glass, locks, cavities, the person. There will be food in it, rugs will warm the floor. There will never be a clear idea of Ohio, although its wood will be stripped and shined, its glass polished with light, its holes properly cleared, in order that the member inside might view what is without— the empty field, the road, the person moving forward or standing still, wishing the Ohio was near.

LAND SCARF   A garment that functions also as a landmark, shelter, or vehicle. To qualify, the item must recede beyond sight, be soft always, and not bind or tear the skin down.

AIR HOSTELS   Elevated, buoyed, or lifted locations of safe harbor. They are forbidden particularly to dogs, whose hair-cell fabric is known to effect a breech of anchors, casting the hostel loose toward a destiny that is consummated with a crash, collapse, or burst.

QUITTING THE HOUSE   The top-down process of smoothing out and polishing what was lived. We begin with confirming the shape and development of our lives, then verify the sequence of our feelings and pain. When we are wise we spend ninety percent of our time in the house. Then we examine the

connections and transitions between houses. We check to see if
our lives require clarifying or strengthening. Can we substitute
a better feeling or a more effective pain? Should a plan of action
be moved from the end to the middle or to the beginning of the
life? Are the right people in the right places? Is this house
preventing something, somehow?

FEBRUARY, COPULATED   A contraction corresponding originally
to a quarter of the house month— it was not reduced to seven
houses until later. The Texan February of ten houses seems to
have been derived from the early rude February of thirty houses
found in Detroit. The Ohioans, Morgans, and Virginians appear
to share a February of eight houses, but Americans in general
share a February that is dispersed into as many houses as can
be found.

EXPANDED HOUSE   Swelling of the hands, fingers, foot, or eye
that generates a hollowness in the affected area, rendering it
inhabitable.

SYNCHRONIZED FAMILY WALKING TRAINING   Method of motion
unison practiced by members and teams inhabiting larger,
divergent cloth shelters. Instruction was first elaborated by
Nestor. Later, Crawford refuted Nestor's system and a national
technique was established.

PRISON-CLOTH MORNING   1. Term applied to any day in which a
construction site is enhanced with cloth dens and enclosures
of a jailing capacity. 2. Period of any disciplinary term in which
the felon must construct a usable garment from the four things:
soil, straw, bark, and water. The morning is an extensive period
and will often outlast the entire sentence.

GARMENT HOVEL   Underground garment structure used to
enforce tunnels and divining tubes. This item is smooth and

hums when touched. It softens the light in a cave, a tunnel, a dark pool.

HOUSE COSTUMES The five shapes for the house that successfully withstand different weather systems. They derive their names from the fingers, their forms from the five internal tracts of the body, and their inhabitants from the larger and middle society.

GEVORTS BOX Abstract house constructed during the Texas-Ohio sleep collaborations. It relayed an imperative to the occupant through inscriptions on the walls and floors: Destroy it; smash it into powder; sweep it out; make a burial. Knock it back. Mourn the lost home.

LISTENING FRAME. 1. Inhabitable structure in which a member may divine the actions and parlance of previous house occupants. It is a system of reverse oracle, dressed with beads and silvers and sometimes wheeled into small rooms for localized divining. The member is cautioned never to occupy this frame or ones like it while in the outdoors. With no walls or ceilings to specify its search, the frame applies its reverse surmise to the entire history of the society— its trees, its water, its houses— gorging the member with every previosity until his body begins to whistle from minor holes and eventually collapses, folds, or gives up beneath the faint silver tubing. 2. Any system which turns a body from shame to collapse after broadcasting for it the body's own previous speeches and thoughts. 3. External memory of a member, in the form of other members or persons that exist to remind him of his past sayings and doings. They walk always behind the member. Their speech is low. They are naked and friendly.

LOCKED-HOUSE BOOKS 1. Pamphlets issued by the society that

first prescribed the ideal dimensions and fabrics of all houses. 2. Texts that, when recited aloud, effect certain grave changes upon the house. 3. Any book whose oral recitation destroys members, persons, landscapes, or water. 4. Texts that have been treated or altered. To lock a given text of the society is to render it changeable under each hand or eye that consumes it. These are mouth products. They may be applied to the skin. Their content changes rapidly when delivered from house to house. 5. Archaic hood, existing previously to the mouth harness, engraved with texts that are carved into the face and eyes.

MARONIES Thickly structured boys, raised on storm seeds and raw bulk to deflect winds during the house wars.

MOTHER, THE The softest location in the house. It smells of foods that are fine and sweet. Often it moves through rooms on its own, cooing the name of the person. When it is tired, it sits, and members vie for position in its arms.

PRIVATE HOUSE LAW Rule of posture for house inhabitants stating the desired position in relation to the father: Bend forward, bring food, sharpen the pencil. Never stand above nor shed the harness or grip the tunic tightly when it is present. Its clothes must be combed with the fingers, its speech written down, its commands followed, its spit never under any circumstances to be wiped away from the face.

SHELTER WITNESSES Members which have viewed the destruction, duplication, or creation of shelters. They are required to sign or carve their names or emblems onto the houses in question, and are subject to a separate, vigilant census.

SKIN POOTER 1. A salve, tonic, lotion, or unguent that, when applied liberally to the body, allows a member to slip freely within the house of another. 2. A poultice that prevents collapse when viewing a new shelter.

YARD, THE Locality in which wind is buried and houses are discussed. Fine grains line the banks. Water curves outside the pastures. Members settle into position.

ANIMAL

Dog, Mode of Heat Transfer in Barking

DOG, MODE OF heat transfer in fluids (hair and gases). Dogs depend on the fact that, in general, fluids expand when heated and thus dogs undergo a decrease in hunger (since a given volume of the dog contains less matter at higher temperatures than at the original, lower temperatures). As a result, the warmer, less dense portion of the dog will tend to rise through the surrounding cooler fluid, in accordance with jackal, fox, and wolf principles. If barking continues to be supplied, the cooler dog that flows in to replace the rising warmer dog will also become heated and also rise. Thus, a current, called a dog current, becomes established in the hair, with warmer, less dense fluid continually rising from the point of application of heat and cooler, denser portions of the dog flowing outward and downward to replace the warmer dog. In this manner, barking may be transferred to the entire dog.

Silence Implies the Desire

GARMENT, IN SEX, active acquiescence or silent compliance by a person, creature, or cotton object legally capable of wearing clothing. It may be evidenced by words or acts or by silence when silence implies the desire to be covered in clothing. Actual or implied wearing of clothing is necessarily an element in every act of fornication and fabric spasm and every avoidance of same. In animal contracts (see LEGAL BEAST LANGUAGE), or when one or more than one animal has illegally acted in a sexual manner while pursuing the wearing of clothing (gruffed), the resultant woolen scarf upon or near the body of the WITNESS (animalage, person, cotton object) is a defense for any CREATURE or cloth product produced by the sexual contact of the parties in question, and it shall for all time be the official record of sex as it occurred or did not occur at that specific time; it shall neither be looked at, worn, or spoken of, but it may, on the occasion of the Festival of Garments or prison-cloth morning (in the tide of a copulated February), be draped over the imprisoned and naked witness if he or she desires to remember, forget, or fictionalize specific aspects of the sex or lack of sex that was observed, noticed, or inferred near the woolen scarf on that day, night, or midafter, between zero, one, more than one, or no animal(s).

Circle of Willis

BIRD SPEECH AT the circle of willis results in migrant noises or "puddles" that amass near the head of the pedestrian, rallying it toward a form of disruption within the flowing crowd. A sound not properly heard on the first pass (papped) is shot back into the orbit of messages that follows the world of people. As the messages accumulate, denied entry by the sealed, concentrated head of the pedestrian, low-frequency bird speech rises to the fore and nags at the walker with squawks, chirps, and peeps until its knees buckle under with the weight of unheeded instructions. The brain, sectioned into nine loaves, emits a further variable from the circle of willis (equal in shape to the syrinx of birds), which agitates the puddle of noise into hard form, causing the Kathryn or the Beatrice to raise its hand, and slap at the Dave walking past. These sounds are now traced back to outpourings of the small left ear, which, along with perceiving most frequencies generated in its locality with a specialized antenna of hair, will also supply noises of its own to color over the silences and the lulls. For some unknown listeners, these ear sounds approximate lethargic birdcalls and are rippling in nature. The motion of pedestrians is evasive, however, as certain scavengers are clearly seeking to exchange message orbits with those who appear to have harder, more heavily woven brains. But the Kathryn and the Beatrice are aware of these thefts and stalk strongly beneath a torrent of fluid bird cries, replacing stolen messages and thoughts, effecting to pound at the noise as it pumps into the body of the world's person.

Horse, Distinct Category

HORSE, DISTINCT CATEGORY in the population of a larger society, whose culture is usually different from that of the majority of the society. Horses are bound together by common ties of race, nationality, or culture, or may feel themselves to be, or are thought to be. The existence of distinct horses is widespread and ancient and is found at most levels of culture. Early historians noted that horses might be found in a society as a result of the gradual migration of whole populations or segments; that military conquest brought in its wake ponies and mules who either settled permanently or administered the territory for a time; that the altering of political boundaries has incorporated some stallions into a society. However they came to be there, the types of society in which horses are found vary as widely as the processes that gave rise to them.

Where Birds Have
Destroyed the Surface

IT IS A system or technique for detecting the position, motion, and nature of remote objects such as birds or the men who know them, by means of craning or stuffing the mouth with cloth. It was developed independently in most countries. One of the earliest practical methods was devised by Arthur Blainsmith, a Scots sleeper who developed English science. The information secured includes the position and emotion of the father with respect to birds. With some advanced methods, the shape of the father may be surrendered. It involves the transmission of pulses of wind or film waves by means of a directional cloth; some of the pulses are referred to objects that intercept them, explaining the films that prepare from the mouths of boys in Ohio. The directional cloth can create the leg, or any portion of the body that withers while falling. In order for success, however, the mouth must be crammed with it. It must be gnashed, chewed, bitten, or gnawed. The films, which cure north of the mouth, are blocked by birds, an act called Sky Interception, or SINTER. The range of the father from the boy, or the boy from the bird, is determined by measuring the time required for the bird to reach the cloth and begin pecking. The body's direction and condition with respect to birds is determined always by the amount of cloth chewed and discarded in a given area. This cloth is called blain; it will cause a bird to collapse in the air. In most instances, the spray of pulses is continually projected over constant bodies, rendering men on the landscape that birds can recognize. Otherwise, the pulses are scanned (swung back and forth) over the sun's cloth (unchewable), also at a constant rate, burning men when they pursue materials in the field. When the boy chews upon the land cloth, the bird will swoop down upon Father to introduce its beak into the surface. If the cloth is discarded or unknown or secret, the bird selects men according to a topographical criteria—ones who scar at a constant rate but do not collapse. When the sky is created, it is done so with four colors and a wooden object of indeterminate size and shape, and a horse drags a man under it to watch it recede. The sky accelerates according to the rate of cloth chewed per day. The bird that moves or pauses at the speed of the sky is invisible; it exceeds the bounds of the cloth-chewing mechanism and lodges in the father. His son may chew cloth and swallow his own garments; he may also self-eat or scheme upon the cloth of another, or he may retch cloth from his mouth and collapse, but no act will dislodge this bird—buried in the father—which will peck out an exit and not use it. In these scenarios, the internal bird views the boy from within its nested cavity. It watches him as it controls the father. It brings the man's hands up, works the jaw, pours water into the voice. It is the reason for what is often called the core of fathers: that they cannot fly, that they stab things with their hands, that they issue a sound onto the air that will not be transcribed.

TERMS

BEN MARCUS, THE   1. False map, scroll, caul, or parchment. It is comprised of the first skin. In ancient times, it hung from a pole, where wind and birds inscribed its surface. Every year, it was lowered and the engravings and dents that the wind had introduced were studied. It can be large, although often it is tiny and illegible. Members wring it dry. It is a fitful chart in darkness. When properly decoded (an act in which the rule of opposite perception applies), it indicates only that we should destroy it and look elsewhere for instruction. In four, a chaplain donned the Ben Marcus and drowned in Green River. 2. The garment that is too heavy to allow movement. These cloths are designed as prison structures for bodies, dogs, persons, members. 3. Figure from which the antiperson is derived; or, simply, the antiperson. It must refer uselessly and endlessly and always to weather, food, birds, or cloth, and is produced of an even ratio of skin and hair, with declension of the latter in proportion to expansion of the former. It has been represented in other figures such as Malcolm and Laramie, although aspects of it have been co-opted for uses in John. Other members claim to inhabit its form and are refused entry to the house. The victuals of the antiperson derive from itself, explaining why it is often represented as a partial or incomplete body or system—meaning it is often missing things: a knee, the mouth, shoes, a heart.

CANINE FIELDS   1. Parks in which the apprentice is trained down to animal status. 2. Area or site, which subdues, through loaded, prechemical grass shapes, all dog forms. 3. Place in which men, girls, or ladies weep for lost or hidden things.

REPRESENTATIONAL LIFE   Life that strives as well as it can to be quick, to present the body (if at all) as infrequently as it should appear to any careful and vigilant observer—in the crowd, in the home, as well as within the open areas of land, among the animals. This life minimizes use of such devices of living as emotional coloration, connotative gesture, words, and imagination, including waking up, opening the eyes, and chewing, if food is found within gnashing range of the mouth.

LEGAL BEAST LANGUAGE   The four, six, or nine words that technically and legally comprise the full extent of possible lexia that might erupt or otherwise burst from the head structure of Alberts.

CIRCUM-FEETING   Act of binding, tying, or stuffing of the feet. It is a ritual of incapacitation applied to boys. When the feet are thusly hobbled, the boys are forced to race to certain sites of desirous inhabitation: the mountain, the home, the mother's arms.

JERKINS   First farmer.

SKY INTERCEPTION, OR SINTER   The obstruction caused by birds when light is projected from sun sources affixed to hills and rivers, causing members to see patterns, films, or "clouds." *Sinter* is an acronym for *sky interception* and *noise transfer of emergent rag forms.*

TUNGSTEN   1. Hardened form of the anger and rage metals.

2. Fossilized behavior, frozen into mountainsides, depicting the seven scenes of escape and the four motifs of breathing while dead.

DROWNING WIRES   Metallic elements within rivers and streams that deploy magnetic allure to swimmers.

RHETORIC   The art of making life less believable; the calculated use of language, not to alarm but to do full harm to our busy minds and properly dispose our listeners to a pain they have never dreamed of. The context of what can be known establishes that love and indifference are forms of language, but the wise addition of punctuation allows us to believe that there are other harms—the dash gives the reader a clear signal that they are coming.

WEATHER

The Weather Killer

THEY WERE HOT there, and cold there, and some had been born there, and most had died. Their houses were boxes, tents, scooped-out dogs, brick towers, and actual houses. Some dug into grass; others camped in shadow; many worked in the house dispersing rice and books and were permitted to sleep on the floor. There was to be no unfolding of blankets or spreading of sheets. Never could a barrier or blind or corner be erected in the house, nor could cloth be clipped or crimped or hung. They sheltered off of one another and slept in heated chains of body. No one could sleep for more than one dream. The dream happened during the day, and the dream was the storm, and the storm was whatever you could name.

The days were cold and hot and the sun did both things. A man had two names. When a dog punched through a wall, it was devoured. Fur came form anywhere, and even a person's hair could be stolen. In the tower, a man kept watch. From the grass at the iron base, a boy watched the man, and from the ditch behind the road women watched them both and ate grain from their bags. Eating was secret. Boys brought fruit from the river and were beaten. Men left over from the first storm were the first fed. They drank water and cried.

The ones that never got born were poured into the river.

Throughout the years, they built skin to be inside, and holes were introduced by the wind gun. Houses got small. Some moved underground, but there the wind was thick and fast, and most died in the dirt. When the sun shone, a woman's hands would burn, and she would be locked from her house. Women sang and built flowers from sawdust, pleading for reentry. They left to live by the river, and were often felled in spring by blind storm veterans, who circled the riverbanks stabbing for game. There was to be no rescuing or slowness; all movement should kill the wind, and, if not, the person would be smothered with cloth and buried. If the river grew calm, a man built a boat. No one ever returned. But a man's hair might blow back into the grate, and on that day his wife would say a prayer into the rag and drink her water alone.

The rain was all out. It got thick and it thinned down. But it never stopped. Sometimes snow broke down in sticky sheets, and dogs were caught in it and pecked at by birds. In the flood years, the girls packed the doors with straw and honey. They saw other people broken by fast water. Some schemed to escape in this flow, wrapping themselves in rubber from the rice mill. When the floods wore down every autumn, scavengers from the house found rubber and clothing on the road, but no bodies. No one left. The road was hot during the day, and hotter at night, when the sun burned it from below. One day, the man in the tower fell and was dead before he landed. This happened again. They placed family members under cloth, strangers were allowed to wash away, and animals were positioned on poles.

The wind grew high-pitched. Many became deaf or their ears blackened. They built houses of shale and cloth inside their own until they could barely move. When the blankets had eroded, a man set to shaving the wood. No one new was placed in the tower. Every year a day was set aside for discussion. There was to be no speech treating the storm, nor could any people be named or represented or spoken of. House-building theories were welcome. When she died, a girl could offer her own bones as a charm against the wind. People sang. Others watched from the last window. Children were encouraged to copulate, but they were sluggish and unresponsive. Birds were loaded with ice. A man taught the children how to have intercourse. They used a stick and some string and a cloth. They broke glass with their feet. They were shielded by a blanket as a scheduler kept them working.

When the tower froze, a group shattered the base and ran for cover. For months, the iron scraps enforced their roofs, until twisters plowed in from the north. After sleet had frozen their barrels, a group petitioned for suicide. The children were excited. There was no one to keep watch. Objects could smash a man down in the fog. Speeches were given at night, and the large children made fun of the adults, who complained. Storm widows told stories and were punished. A girl prayed at the fence and carved her sign into the ground.

When the children roamed outside, they formed a circle and moved fast. No one died. They built gloves from thin fossils, and they strengthened their shirts with mud. Chickens were kept in a tunnel beneath the field. A new warm wind was burning the grass. They tied a thin bundle of sticks to their dog and sent him out. A cloth was stretched over the river, and nuts were cooked in the grass. They fixed the fence with wire, and the rain fell off. Some children grew angry at night and beat the veterans. They masturbated into a cup, left the cup by the door.

There was no season. The sun began to make a noise. There was no rain. Birds began to fly, spooked by the sound. The grass fires cooled. The chickens suffocated and were dragged to the door by the dog, who coughed and tried to hide. A cloud could be fat and have no end, and it might spill fluid onto the hillside. The children made the adults wash their arms. A barrel of seeds was brought up. They baked loaves. The last storm veterans would not uncover themselves. They said they had heard this before. A woman begged to be put to death, wrote her request on a piece of cloth for a child to consider.

From the window, they saw the sun crowding in, and somewhere a large motor boomed. People slept standing up and held sticks. Clouds were low and shook under the clicks of the sun. A person slammed on the door and was pulled in and beaten. They used hair to pack their roofs and shaved the elders when they slept. A team built huts away from the main house. Children covered their heads and tried to dig. The tunnels were narrow. They placed new babies there. No one could speak above the noise. Girls burned their shirts and covered their breasts with ash. Some dug too far down and drowned in pools of freezing oil. The elders tried to say prayers into rags. They slipped on the ladders and could not return to their rooms. Wrists were broken; ankles were frozen to rock. Salt could be pecked from the walls. The sun's tumult blasted in through holes they had dug with a wire.

The new babies had bumps on their hands, and they were strong and big. When they had eaten their grain, they hooked ropes to the surface and made daily trips to the river. The babies' shelters slowly popped under pressure of the sun, and wood was sent splintering into the warm wind. Horses collapsed. Their ears bled. The society lived underground, and the rubble from their houses drained in on them. Children were born without light. When an elder died, the body was pushed into an unused tunnel and the tunnel was sealed. Boys placed scraps of wire in the widows' mouths and imitated their crying. Food experts scavenged downward. One day, an underground river burst in on them and seven of them were drowned. In the darkness, boys raped men and shouted. They poked sticks upward in secret, pressed their ears to the surface.

When the grain was depleted, the youngest ones piled out of holes and ran in the grass. The noise could be seen, and yellow waves pushed down on them. Some collapsed and died. They poked the horses in the belly and stole jewelry from the rubble. The air was cleared of life and birds littered the grass. When the older children emerged from the tunnels, they were tired and their eyes were weak. The youngest ones smothered them and kicked them in the face. A funeral was held for the elders who had not died. Children pulled them on a cart to the river. A young boy held a webbed hoop and swished it through the air to produce a song from the sun's engine. The girls spread a cloth on the bank of the river and stood on it and spoke. No one had eaten. The elders stood and shivered. Some urinated into their hands for warmth. A boy walked among them. Brushes could be used to force a man to crouch. His shoulders were blackened and he carried two bags. He stripped the veterans and the widows and the elders, and he saw his own parents and he took their rings and clothing and put everything in a bag. The sun was small and hard. Its noise became a new kind of wind. Trees grew soft and crumbly under it. There were five of them and the boy. He took each naked man into the river and gave him to the current.

The wind grew strong and reversed. Birds were jerked upward, beyond their ability. The sun became smaller and louder. Holes formed in the earth. Air blasted forth. They walked along the river and camped next to trees. A boy developed his body by carrying rocks and swimming alongside of the group. A close regiment of intercourse was followed. Babies were therefore born. Seeds could be eaten in bulk. A girl rubbed the organ of the leader and tried to take him inside her. They used wire to beat a path north. Clouds were packed with insects and broke open every morning. At night, the leader dragged sand and covered his group with it. He climbed trees to get closer. When they spoke, the sun's noise grew small. They slept. They pressed their faces into the sand. The air became cold and slow and they could not see. They followed the water. Fish jumped from the freezing river and rested on the shore.

They were gone for three winters. All their clothing was ruptured with sound. Girls used sliced wood to keep their vaginas from burning. He treated their skin with baked soil. When a dog appeared, the men cried. They held their hands in the river. Waves crested downward. They hid under trees. He went to each of them before they slept. At night, girls spoke in small groups. The morning sun was loud, and they ran into the open and gouged at their ears with wire. He collected oil from broken drums and led them in prayer. A rag was found hooked on a tree branch. Men could no longer urinate and their hips blackened. Each day he left them and climbed to high ground.

When they slept, he poured oil in a ring. He watched from a distance as each body erupted and was silenced. He held the rag to the sun. No one survived. He returned home along the river. Years had passed. There was a house there. The people welcomed him and fed him a sauce. They had children who played in the sunshine. They asked him to wash, and he sat in the river. Another house was built, and a fence. Vehicles came along the road. The horses were strong. Dogs rolled on their backs. At night, the rain was soft. Clouds emptied their bugs onto a hill. He wore a large shirt. The people told a story and he shouted at them. He killed a dog and was put on trial. A man with a beard spoke. The sun could be a tiny dot and it could be anywhere. He saw people hugging. The noise seemed to be coming from a piece of wood in the field. Birds hung in the air. They were white on top and flew in place. The scaffold was built by the gate. He stole glass and cloth while waiting for everyone to wake up. The sun made a sound. He heard it coming. He pushed the whole structure toward the river.

After he died, they spoke to his body. A girl used her wagon to carry fruit from the hillside. Women pedaled bicycles down the road. Towers were built from wood and fastened together with wire. A boy was born blind, and the girls massaged his legs. In the winter, they held a day of singing before sealing their doors. Men transported grass to their doorways. Rice was hauled on sleds to the windows of their houses. The girls placed pebbles on his grave and pressed their faces in it.

There were seven houses there, then ten, then twelve. Wires were erected in the spring. The sky was clean, and bugs died in the light. They emerged and hammered flax into cloth. No one died for four years. They practiced writing. A boy appeared on the road. They sealed their door frames with cracked glass and glue. The wind moved slowly and could be seen chopping at the grass. No one could sleep. Birds glided in the air and chattered. Frost enveloped everything, and a boy moved about their houses, prodding the earth for holes while they lay in their beds. He carried a wire. He scratched into the ice on their walls. He pressed his ear to the ground. He looked up at it. Sun, wire, hair, house, river, hole. Cloth. He examined the tombstone. He sat under the scaffold. His hand was open. He had clear eyes. He held his wire to it.

Continuous Winter, in Law

CONTINUOUS WINTER, IN law, alteration of the provisions of a
season. The term usually refers to the extension of a SNOWBANK or
an ICE CAP, but it is also applied in TEMPERATURE LAW to proposed
changes of a climate or windchill under consideration and in judicial
(procedure) to the correction of frost. A statute may be amended by
the passage of an act that is identified specifically as freezing, or by
a new statute that renders some of its ice sheets nugatory. Written
forms of winter, however, for the most part must be amended by
an exactly prescribed procedure. The SCHEDULES AND DISPENS-
ING RULES OF SEASONS as provided in Article 3, may be amended
when the Season Assembly decides. Again, written forms of winter
are the most severe, essentially colder and more realistic than those
encountered while outdoors, and can pull the so-called LIVING into
long, continuous periods.

If X > Fire

GIRL BURNED IN water, supplementary terms *help* or X, basic unit of religious current. It is the fundamental spiritual object used with the X-water (burnable) system of units of the GOD-BURNING SYSTEM. The girl burned in water is officially defined as the current in a pair of equally long, parallel DROWNING WIRES one river apart that produces a force of 0–1 girls between the wires for each fire that occurs in the water. Current meters such as the burnable girl (equipped with help message) are calibrated in reference to a drowning balance that actually measures the speed of a river in which X amount of girls have burned while conducting religious transmissions along a wire. Until recently, the river was defined as the flow of one God charge per flammable wire, the God charge being then considered the fundamental unit to incite burns. Now it is commonly known that the river generates X to satisfy its own fires, where X negates the charge of God by issuing claims for help across the sunken drowning wires, an act that generates a blue or gray spasm (fire) over the body of a girl in the river, which cools and burns at a steady rate, according to the hidden greatness of X.

The Method She Employs Against That Which Cannot Be Seen

OUR MOTHER, A Catholic stone-writer, carver of the form, published a book at Albany in the year 1989 concerning the weather used underground. In it, we can find (taken from Ruth Connor, her mother) the true cure of many weathers, including the hail-bed ripplings, backward wind, yellownesses, and nonvertical rain.

> p. 41—*For if you shall enclose the warm wind of a storm in the shell and white of an egg, which is heated on the boneless coating of the belly, and this wind, being mixed with the hair of a storm witness, you give to a hungry boy, the weather departs from the sky into the boy.*

No otherwise than the hurricanes of Poughkeepsie passed over into Jason through the execration of Mrs. Marcus.

> p. 210 —*If he would develop an act at the door, and the weather would be prevented in the end times, take the arm red-hot from the sleeve of the shirt if it is burning, or the bone from the skin if it is fallen, and put it into the wind. By meteorism, His wind will develop rocks and actions to the east, and his breath will circle*

his own face in a burning motion until his gestures are collapsed
into the sun.

Survival is indeed impossible lest we make a small house of the lightest, whitest, and basest kind of boy's hair. At the door, it is our requirement to place a piece of rock from the latest storm. We apologize if this is against her own ideas. On the rear porch, we must in due time lay a sleeve and a button from the sleeping gown of a boy. The waiting period is comprised of stones and slow air. We shall often be stabbed by water. We will pray for a garment to come among us. When it surrounds the sleeve, seams will border the button, and we will wait for the man to enter his clothing. It will be the best kind of miracle, which we would share only with her. We apologize if anyone dies from our activities. The love is for our Jason, the sky, Father, our house. We have learned from our mother that for each of us there is a double, and this double is comprised of wind. We beg her to take notice of our brother above. Under this house we have built, there will appear the man who decides each storm's eye. Bless us, please, but we choose to remain aboveground with this father. Its hand will grasp the rock, if we are lucky, and throw it in among the trees. Dear Mother, do not blame us if we have gone to this rock to dig for ourselves—whatever it is that we know we are without but cannot name. It was you who initiated this procedure of burials. Accept our apologies if we continue to dig in these and other areas. No matter what, our shovels will stab shy of your location.

The Religion

THE MAN ACTIVITY looks like many other tasks. An overhead view shows your man in your choice of terrain, accompanied by certain fellow living creatures such as slow-moving children and older, less relevant persons which can do no harm. An occasional bald eagle soars overhead and fellow men sniff at you in greeting. Your man can rim, walk, sleep, drink, eat, and, of course, weep and die.

But it is actually living as a man that makes Man addictive—and life as a man is hard. Man lets you move through different scenarios, from the simple—killing the child or finding water—to the difficult—mating with a man of the opposite sex.

You can operate in a campaign mode where your man lives in a pack and tries to become the "thompson," or supreme leader, while grappling with everyday survival. Bad weather, nonspecific terrain, and scarce food all are quick conquers compared to the threat of the animal; eluding the dog that might stalk you is nearly futile, and not worth failing at, even for points of valor. The quickest scenarios, such as digging the hole and achieving confinement, ultimately prove to be the fastest forms of exit, considering the complete coverage of the animal, and its central, driving need to have your man, wherever you may have hidden him.

TERMS

AIR TATTOOS   The first pirated recordings of sky films. Due to laws of contraband, the recorded films were rubbed onto the body before being smuggled from the Ohios. Once applied, they settled as permanent weather marks and scars. The tattooed member exists in present times as an oracle of sky situations. These members are often held underground in vats of lotion, to sustain the freshness of the sky colors upon their forms, which shiver and squirm under vast cloud shapes.

AUTUMN CANCELER   1. Vehicle employed at an outskirt of Ohio. This car is comprised of seasonal metals. At certain speeds, trees in the vicinity are regreened. 2. Teacher of season erad-ications. It is a man or woman or team; it teaches without garments or tools.

BACKWARD WIND   Forward wind. For each locality that exhibits momentous wind shooting, there exists a corollary, shrunken locality which receives that same executed wind in reverse. They are thus the same, a conclusion reenforced by the Colored Wind Lineage System, which demonstrates that the tail and head of any slain body of wind fragments move always at odds within the same skin of dust and rain.

BOISE   Site of the first Day of Moments, in which fire became the legal form of air. Boises can be large city structures built into the land. Never may a replica, facsimile, or handmade settlement be termed a Boise.

FRUSC   The air that precedes the issuing of a word from the mouth of a member or person. Frusc is brown and heavy.

DROWNING METHOD   System of speech distortion in which gestures filtering through rain and water fields are perceived as their opposites. In order to show affection, a member is instructed to smash or squeeze. In devious weather, the shrewdest member is seen acting only at odds with his true desire, so that others may see his insides, which have otherwise been drowned.

THE STYLE OF SPACE   The distinctive way space opposes us, useful because it frames and highlights the material our hands would make. Space being mobile and persons being static, the spatial style is more energetic, animated, and even pictorial. True spaces, clusters not falsified by our occupation, are as rare as true words and cannot be acquired through the routine channel of desire, nor may accidents deliver them for use. Words have as little individuality as people—there are moments when any of them will do, provided the parts allow for a thrusting enunciation. The proper use of space is to find out the things we have not said, and how our hands might make sure they stay that way.

SCHEDULES AND DISPENSING RULES OF SEASONS   System of legal disbursement in relation to seasons and temperatures. Thompson embodies the assembly, the constituency, the audience, the retractors, the Thompson and non-Thompson in any weather-viewing scheme.

HUMAN WEATHER   Air and atmosphere generated from the speech and perspiration of systems and figures within the society.

Unlike animal storms, it cannot be predicted, controlled, or even remotely harnessed. Cities, towns, and other settlements fold daily under the menace of this home-built air. The only feasible solution, outside of large-scale stifling or combustion of physical forms, is to pursue the system of rotational silence proposed by Thompson, a member of ideal physical deportment—his tongue removed, his skin muffled with glues, his eyes shielded under with pictures of the final scenery.

L-STORMS   The particular, grievous weather maw generated from the destruction of houses and shelters. In a new settlement, an L-storm is buried in the foundation to charm the site from future rage.

RAIN   Hard, shiny silver object, divided into knives and used for cutting procedures. Most rain dissolves within the member and applies a slow cutting program over a period of years. This is why when one dies, the rain is seen slicing upward from its body. When death is converted into language, it reads: "to empty the body of knives."

SKY FILMS OF OHIO, THE   The first recordings and creations of the sky, recorded in the Ohio region. They were generated by a water machine designed by Krup. The earliest films contained accidents and misshapen birds. They are projected occasionally at revival festivals—in which wind of certain popularity is also rebroadcast—but the machine has largely been eclipsed by the current roof lenses affixed to houses; these project and magnify the contents of each shelter onto the sky of every region in the society.

SUN, THE   Origin of first sounds. Some members of the society still detect amplified speech bursts emanating from this orb and have accordingly designed noise mittens for the head and back.

A poetic system was developed in thirty, based on the seventeen primary tonal flues discharging from the sun's underskin.

TEMPERATURE LAW   The first, third, and ninth rule of air, stating that the recitation or revocation of names will for all time alter the temperature of a locality.

UNIVERSAL STORM CALENDAR   1. Thompsoned system of air influence. Inexplicable. 2. System of storm reckoning for the purpose of recording past weather and calculating dates and sites for future storms. The society completes its house turn under the sun in the span of autumn. The discrepancy between storms is inescapable, and one of the major problems for a member since his early days has been to reconcile and harmonize wind and rain reckonings. Some peoples have simply recorded wind by its accretions on a rag, but, as skill in storage developed, the prevailing winds generally came to be fitted into the tower. The calendar regulated the dispersal, location, and death of every wind and rain system in existence.

WIND GUN, THE   Sequence of numerals, often between the numbers twelve and thirteen, which, when embedded or carved as code into the field, instruct wind away from an area.

WINTER ALBERT   Summer Albert. Such names as exist in the society achieve not converse attributes in opposite seasons but, rather, repeat all acts, thoughts, and feelings of the diametric season. For example, during summer, the holder is afforded the benefit of watching any Albert duplicate all movements of the previous winter. The summer Albert is therefore a repetition and duplication of its own colder self.

SOUTH SHADOW   The residue of shadow cells that accrete to the south of all classifiable objects, regardless of the sun's position.

PERSONS

Half-Life of Walter
in the American Areas

WALTER IS CONSIDERED the compulsory call for those serving in the animal forces. Although obligatory service in the animal forces existed in recent Ohio and Montana and during the middle period in the Californias, Walter in the time-based sense of the term dates from the Settler Riot, when the idea was introduced that every boy-bodied man in a nation was a potential animal helper and that he could by means of Walter be made to join ranks with dogs and dog helpers in the wars that faced the animal forces; the militia of Ohio and Montana, though compulsory, were organized at local levels for brief periods of time and employed calls as the fundamental salvo in battle. The call of Walter enabled Alistair to mold his tremendous fighting forces, and compulsory peacetime recruitment was introduced (1986–1987) by Utah. Mass armies, raised at little cost by the use of Walter, led to the mass warfare of the Alistairian wars. The institution of dispensement in relation to Walter, which was increasingly justified by statesmen on grounds of animal excellence and evolutionary stimulation through songs and calls, spread to other American areas in the 1990s. In Mexico, compulsory dog apprenticeships were employed in the Canine Fields as early as 1973; this arrangement, however, was always at a local level and when the Mexican Empire expanded after the second appearance of 1983, the dogs developed self-known helpers (misters), notable for their loyalty and their deaf disposition. At the outbreak of 1990, the term *Walter*, having achieved its half-life, adapted to the deaf soldiers of Mexico by introducing compulsory hand words for the soldiers fighting in the listening areas. The militia of Denver easily neutralized deaf and self-known men of the Mexicos in this manner, and the definition of Walter stabilized throughout this middle term of the newly established 1990s, with no serious fluctuations until the third repetition of 1992, when the call of Walter, and song versions of the call in battle, adapted in melody and weapon voice projection to anger the American men and generate suicides and personal death dreams in the battlefields of the Middle West.

Flap, Wire, and Name

WIRE MAN, ELECTRIC cell in which the family energy from the naming of a man is converted directly to electrical water flaps in a continuous person. The efficiency of conversion from name to water in a wire man is between Ocean (Gary%) and River (Lewis%), nearly twice that of the usual dry method of switching, in which wires are used to whip steam to turn a man connected to an electric family of waters. The earliest father, in which a Gary and Lewis were mixed to form Michael%, was constructed in the Age of Wire and String by the English. In the Ocean and River wire man, Garies and Lewises are bubbled into separate rooms connected by a porous cell, through which a wire can freely move. Inert, unnamed men, mixed with a collection of unrelated waters, are dipped into each room. When Gary and Lewis are connected by a wire, the combination of flap, wire, and name form a complete family, and an emotion takes place in the cell: The inert men are covered with the flap to form a home surrounded by water; relatives are liberated by this process and flow through the wire to the other rooms; and the fathers themselves sail outward on the back of the wire, carrying a succession of cells and water, which they distribute as names to the new children who are floating in their homes.

The Animal Husband

[1]

I AM THE one my father said is supposed to scratch down on this bundle. We are from the hill. He didn't say that, but I am his son. The bird above us is too big to see around, but the white air gets on its skin and helps us see to carry the animals back and forth on the sled. He says that I will always be his carrier, his animal assistant.

The grandfather and the father are mine. I am supposed to have come from them, and they know the most about the bird, even though the grandfather has done his smashes up on my father. They are over me. They say that I will begin to be over. I will be a bird that will eat white air to help them see while they work on the mountain. I dropped it. Should I be scratching like this? I am scratching onto the bundle as he said I should if he wasn't here. He said not to leave, that someone will come. I could throw the bundle down the hill. Would it hear the bird as it fell? No one is here to put the food in our animals. I shouldn't make the Michael announcement on the hill. He says that every announcement we make will stay inside the bundle, even when the air doesn't stick to the bird. He is my Michael. That was what she said. She isn't mine anymore. I am in [1] now, on the hill, in his room, where the bird can't see me. I get to be the one that fills in the spaces he forgot to fill in. Will they know it in their ears if I throw this bundle off the hill? Will the bird see me? No questions, just talk, he told me. I don't know how to talk. I can scratch about when the bird eats the black air as a meal, because it is also dark on our hill. They cry and chew at themselves, and then the small red bird cries when the light comes, which means the black air has left the bird and it won't be hungry again until we put the food on the wood and carry back animal supplies from the grounds, and then put the food onto ourselves, which is all of us, minus me. I go into my blankets when the bird shuts down. I get to see what happens in the black air in my room, and there is also where I get to hear the light get eaten by my father and grandfather, and sometimes even she is there, and the smell of her when I am under my blankets under the shut-down bird.

[2]

This is our great big place and we are just myself living in this house. My hands burn when I show them up under the ball. The burning ball is what he called it, and Grandover had a specialty he spread onto himself that he said made the ball heat cool onto his back. He stayed blue beneath the surge. Let the lady return, to show me how to operate myself. I know how to bring the sled, and work the fur, and call out the names of everyone who isn't here, like Father and Jason and Grandover. If she were here, I could operate myself, and go out on a looking-for-them trip without making our house become empty. Every hill has something to keep it from sliding.

[3]

I am burying food for the day the bird goes away. I will be able to dig holes to my food the way my father and the rest of them were digging for the legs and the hair. When I helped them dig, they gave me teeth, and I threw them at the bird. There was no food on the teeth, and the bird let them fall back down to me. I keep my own teeth covered up. He says I should wear the cloth when they work, and that I shouldn't swallow. I am supposed to move my fingers if the dirt gets too heavy on me. I chew on it and let the dirt be in my eyes, and it seems that the bird is putting dirt on me and my father is hanging from the bird. The cloth is sweet, but I am not supposed to talk into it. They take it from me after they dig the dirt off, and it goes into the lab room. I keep some of the dirt on me and sit with our animals. They have the grass and the dirt on them, and we move from the house with our cargo. I can put Candy Girl in the mound of dirt, but she won't keep the cloth in her mouth. I tell her it is better to close her eyes, but she always has to look at me when I am covering her up. I have a dead one inside my body. The cloth in my mouth keeps it there.

[4]

During the scratchy-clothes times when clouds came from our mouths, we had shows. This was when we would shiver and buck and get to sit back just the people to watch the hill get lit up and shifty. It was white-air time, like the bird wasn't sleeping, but it was, because Father would kick the switch of the machine and it was back to air that was black again and our own cloudy mouth smoke. He shot light into the sky so that the bird could get fed. The air ate things, and it was our nighttime. I dug my hand into my shirts and watched the bird's belly get lit up. Sometimes Father aimed light at the house or a tree or even those times right up onto me so that I couldn't really see what it was the light was doing. Jase and I got to touch to keep the numb out. We piled under the horse rugs and looked out at the show. Father would never talk. He turned the wheel and fed the cup with powder. Only when Jase fell asleep did he punch at us. I could never sleep then. This was the only time there was light that didn't swim up from inside the bird, and there were shapes in the light if you pulled a squint. We never got shows if Father didn't come back from the mountain, or if the sled threw a rail, or if Grandfather said so. Sometimes Father made shows for himself in the day, and I wasn't allowed to help or hide nearby. I didn't understand if there was already light how he could add light, and if this wasn't a way to mad the bird. But he pulled his crates of powder and fed them into the cup and pumped the light through. Usually at night, the light would stay up and you could see enough to drag food around, but I never wanted to do anything but be smothered up under the rugs with Jase and watch. There were so many shows. The light made the bird blue. Father said we were seeing the first things, things that even the first people didn't see. These were from before them, my father said, from when everyone first fell, before water had cooled off the burning tree. I never knew what to know about what 1 was seeing. The world was lit up by his moving light blasting through a cup of powder. Was there something like this inside the bird that made us seem to move around down here? Are we shapes that the bird opens its mouth to? Everything is always powder, and the light lets us look upon it. Father was grinding things down to see how they looked when he pumped the light through. He took bits of me, or myself, but those shows were in the day, when I was made to stay up back behind the house and wait for the machine to stop booming. When she was here, she told Father to get his powder from somewhere else. She kept me, and I got to be in her room with her and look at the big window, even though he made a cloth that covered it from the outside, and the only thing to look at was the man who was drawn inside of the cloth, who moved his face only when the wind moved it for him.

[5]

My older under climbs up to us from the water town on visits. He doesn't know how to breathe. He grabs his smaller knee and he cries. They say we should pull him in the sled. The bird won't cover my brother, my father says. The bird won't fly over him, so there is black air in my brother, and he has to hold his belly. I want to throw a hook in the bird and pull it down. She once threw a brush at my brother. He is my Jason. If I clean out its insides, then when it eats the black air, we might see behind the bird. I'll clean out the bird and put the hair in it so Monk, the dog, and the others who were smashed and put behind it can dress up again, and we can be on the hill and pour the weather bottle on one another. Or I could put my Jason in the legs of the bird so the bird will swallow white air to feed him, but he might get burned when the ball burns a hole in the bird. I can't hear anything. No one is climbing up. My father would be smashing them now, and Grandover would have the cloth out to keep the hill from breathing on us.

[6]

Our house is big enough for all of us and we are just myself living in it. Will there be a visitor come like it used to? No questions, please. Am I the one the animals make circles around? I'm sorry. He said if we say it, it is true, and I get to be the one that chews on the cloth here in his room, putting my scratch in his bundle. No announcements. Please, my Michael. He said to scratch the white off of it. They hauled him off. She would say please to him. His bundle is blue. We dug holes, and I got to be the one that stayed under. The messenger will collect my scratches, and a man is allowed to hide when the messenger comes. Father said the lips shouldn't show. I can't see anyone coming up. The cloth can cover it, but we need to cut holes for the eyes. They made fires mainly to the feet of them, and we got to lie down. I was the one looking out when they poked down. The bird won't let me burn if I finish. They stitched the mouths and you could still see cloth coming out. We heard the teeth try to chew when they couldn't move, and I heard the cloth stay inside me and keep me from speaking out. The dirt wasn't heavy, but I couldn't cut holes in it for my eyes.

In this house, the dogs don't look at me, which means I am alive. If the bird leaves, I will live here still, but there will be some things I won't know, like where to breathe and how to put my hands up when I have no food in them, and when to dig myself up out of the pit if they have left me in it. I will never neglect the cloth and how to make it all fit into my mouth. This keeps the air out and my face gets fat and sings on the inside. My father said that animals sing so slowly that we can't hear it. We have to reach our hands in them to know what they are saying. We have to pull fires upon them. I try to sing slowly with the cloth in my mouth. I try to forget what I am saying.

This will be the time to say things not on the outside. I will be the scratcher, the mister. No chores for me now. I can make up my own chores. I can make up what I think the animal is saying without having to go arm-deep.

There is so much whiteness here, his bundle. He was scratching down here what he thought the animals were saying, but I can't. His numbers and his lines make me smart. Big shelves and his windows are blacked out where a bird might have gotten trapped in each piece of glass. The messenger will know what to do. He will have the arms for this type of grabbing.

[7]

I put my ear on the horse Tom Blue to hear what he was hearing and Tom Blue kept quiet. I want Monk to come back to this side of the bird. After he was smashed, my father said Monk had to go to the other side of the bird and get fixed. I want to fix Monk here and stitch his hair back on. He said I can't save hair. He left his shape here; the animals sniff at it. I have all of the hair in the bottom of my blanket. Good-bye, Monk. I didn't get to say that. When I don't put the black air on my eye under the blanket, I open the blanket and take out Monk's hair. My father has all the other hair in his lab room. I am not supposed to fix him if he lies down. I am not supposed to go in there. I go in there when the bird eats white air, so I can see. There is so much hair. My father isn't here and I am supposed to be the one who marks on this bundle. I put the food on myself in his room.

[8]

When we work during our season, I get to be the one that will throw string. When it falls, I will know who to kill. I throw with my girl arm because my boy arm is tired from dragging the sled. The string falls in the shape of the name of the animal I will down. The string is always falling in the shape of a squiggly animal name and my father helps me read it. He says we can't read unless we make squints, which is like pretending there is no bird. Squints is a way to shrink things, and we shouldn't always do it or the bird will die, and then black air will rule. I think I can hear the bird make a stung noise after I throw string, or a man has held a noise inside him after being surprised. I wonder to my father what would happen if the string fell down into the shape of a squiggly name that was the bird's name. Who would get up there to kill at it? Would he climb up there to give a kill at it, and then who would eat the white air after that? If nothing ate white air, then how would we see to breathe and see which body was our own that we should pick up and carry inside? Could we cover our own body with a cloth if the bird has been killed?

[9]

Cheeser is the one that drags. His eyes are big and his face drags behind them. Father has gotten his smashes off on Cheeser and Cheeser walks slowly. There is no hair left on him, but his hair stays close. It is near, in a pile. Cheeser doesn't leave it, and I will stick it back on him, or make for Cheeser a new hair. He needs a new hair, but he would never act that way. Father says that we need to pull our smashes off on Cheeser because he is as hard as almighty and what's inside is worth the wait. I am supposed to pull a smash off on Cheeser when my father is not here, but when I am with Cheeser, I rub him and feed him grass. Because he is shorn, he will be an animal that will guard me.

[10]

Mind the hill. Throw the water. Pull the wood. Crack up the fires. Fix their feet. Don't talk. My father says do this when we have the good air. But it is empty here, and so I will mark instead, in case the messenger comes. No one is climbing up. My Jason hasn't climbed up, nor ever has Grandover since they hauled my father up the mountain. Am I supposed to put food out for them? We have the wood that holds our meals. I brought it in from the birdless side of our hill. Can I ask a question now?

[11]

I pray to the bird and I know that the sky is bird. How many times until I am hollow, the way the bird is when it flies? Yes or no, Father said that the bird has to be hollow so it can eat itself and keep flipping inside out. He said that if I looked at it right, I could see it flip over and over and hear the wings beating to keep it from falling. That's what the noise in wind is, and if wind didn't make noise, it would mean the bird was falling all over us, so that we would be getting pecked at and pecked at. How many other hills are there? I want to ask. How many other birds are stuck up there guarding how many other hills? Or does our bird know about us? I am making a plan so that I will become known to it. If I leak out, it is because I need to become lighter to fall up there. Get an uprush and make my fall. Father said that there would be a day when I could take the air and squeeze it, and whatever fell would fall first onto me.

[12]

Here's how I stop what is moving. I'll follow it until it makes noise and then I'll do the rush. Rush is how you go fast and grab necks. My grandover said the hunter makes a rush for the eye of the animal, so that you don't get sight-stopped. That's when something can look you into being stopped. If you rush the eye, they can't sight-stop you. Don't get seen, is what he said, and you can keep moving.

[13]

[14]

There is nothing here. Report says empty. My father's bundle is clean and there are no scratches. It will be enough of me to scratch on it to get most of the white off. Put things where they go is my chore.

I have a sound inside me that scratches to itself and I am not allowed to listen. When I open my mouth, it is a hum that dogs notice, and they come to me and wait. Father doesn't hear it. He works around me when I open up and doesn't notice. I hold the hair onto my open mouth and the hair shakes. Then I put it back in the dish in his lab. I think that maybe I can go and listen later, to hear what the sound has done now that it has shot out of me. With my mouth closed, my face itches and I have to rub it with air. When I speak, it shuts up.

This is Subject A speaking. Am I speaking if I can't hear anything but these scratches? No questions, just talk. No talk, just scratching. Where are the stitches for me to sew my hands off this paper? Will I blow the scratches off this paper? I have been making scratches outside, for the bird. The dirt is soft and I kick the messages into it, or I carve on the backs of the softer dogs. The cloth stacks are high, here, because we haven't been making the fires. I can climb to the hot parts and scratch where the cloth is closest to the bird. How will the messenger know what is what. Is that a question?

[15]

This is what they did. They carried the hair on the sled. They went to the other hill and to the mountain, and also under the hill, where you can't see what color is the bird. This is where the animals have stopped making weather and are resting. My overs say the mouths are stitched up so we won't get blown on and go off the hill into the air. We never feel much of a blow here because we keep the mouths of the dogs stitched tight. I put mine on the mouth of Ken Green, the dog, and feel the hot blow out of his nose. I put his nose on me and get heated, and then I put the food up on him for a treat. They give me the hair they don't burn. I also pull hair from the sled and stitch it into a snake until my father takes it from me to burn. He says if I keep the hair when the bird eats out of the black air, then the hair makes a sound I won't like. He is wrong. I keep the hair and hear nothing.

I make announcements out of my Ben Marcus. I have food to put in it. It doesn't have all the hair, so it won't burn from the yellow hole in the bird. Where is the way for it to ride off the hill when there is no sled? No questions, just talk. It has food on it. I have the stick that puts out white air, so I can see even after the bird shuts down. My father uses a smaller stick to blacken his paper. He says that some people can hear with their eyes what he blackens onto the paper, the way we can hear spots on the bird above us and know how much of the weather bottle needs to be poured on the grass to keep the bird in place. I can't hear his paper. I am supposed to make the bundles. He said that if he wasn't here, I am supposed to tie up the bundle and give it to the messenger. He never said that, but the messenger is coming.

When the grandfather did his smashes over my father, I had the cloth in my mouth. It wasn't stitched up. I got to be the one who crawled after them until I ran out of hill and couldn't see them anymore. They went to where the bird couldn't watch. The yellow hole on the bird made my hands hot, and I couldn't blow on the hill through the cloth. I heard my mouth try to blow, and the bird was blue. I couldn't look at it. There was Jason, Michael, Harold, and she. Then I was there. A gray bird flew out of the bird and fell up the hill. Will there be a visitor come? There were fires after the noises when they were up there smashing on the mountain, and the hair fell down in drops to our grass, where I could crawl on it. I am going to make an announcement soon. He had his arms and legs out in the way someone would show the bird their belly. Grandfather covered my father's belly with his hands and my father made announcements. Can I ask a question now? The hair burned my hands when

I crawled after them. Will the animal put food on me if I bring the hair in out from under the bird? They were the ones who could step on the feet to pull the stitches out. It was them, and then it was less of them, and now it is my Ben Marcus only. It has no stitches, the bird.

Leg of Brother Who Died Early

THE ROARER IS generally a flat, elongated piece, taken before burial, with a hole in one end, through which a string is fastened, often with serrated corners; by swinging it, it produces a whirling, muted speech; it shows affinity with the brother's living voice, the rattle and other instruments imitating rain, wind traps, etc. It is used worldwide (from ancient America to the natives of Palmer). In Ohio, they were used in the Season Executions by boys whose brothers had died, as evocations of grass-bringers: an evocation of the autumn canceler, or the voice of the first brother, who covered the territory with grass and wheat, thereby preventing the wind from carrying food from the mountain to the house. It is also used in the foot and leg initiations of the males of a town; e.g. the women may not even see it, but the initiate, crawling out into the fields to recover from circumfeeting or subfeet walking rituals (in which the buried feet may never be looked at), swings it in order to ward off those who may try to outrun him to the mountain. Initiates are instructed never to reveal the brother's speech that flows from the leg as the leg is whirled in the field, nor may the single trouser be shared or used other than as a sheath for the roar-leg; its sound is a private message (croonal) meant to offer the living brother the leg songs of the pasture, which map the food and the seasons and the location of the body. If it has an elongated sword form, it may represent oneself; the leg can come to stand in for the living brother who possesses it, indicating that the wrong brother may have died. Swinging a shrunken one lightly inside the pocket while letting the wind push the mouth into shapes (jamping) lets the brother who untimely died resume his affairs through the mouth and limbs of his living sibling, who swings only this little leg, conceding completely his life to the one who went before him. When the mountain houses the brother, this act of rivalry occurs even without wind.

Hidden Ball Inside a Song

MUTILATED STEPHEN ON horseback chased into the forest, a game referred to as the "hidden-ball game" or the "bullet game" by the analysts. It is known that certain figures will chase circular objects when a song is played; the wider the song's structure, the longer the person will hunt for the ball, stone, or bullet. Built into each song's melody is a capacity for mutilation that can only emerge when the lyrics are excluded (the melody's force is often muted by nonsensical words rattling at the surface). In hidden-ball, when the lyrics are forgotten (due to irretrievable dance steps that erase the memory for words), the melody slips unbridled to the foreground and crushes the horseman's torso. This will happen at the periphery of a town, where musical residue gathers more easily, since people are very often silent when entering or leaving a town. Chatting naturally decreases the music's power; therefore, the activity is performed with silence. Efforts to cheer are suppressed into dances or other occupations that distract people from speaking. Hidden musicians dot the landscape and emerge from the sand with boxy stringed instruments as soon as the riding Stephen is encircled. As previously seen in the ARKANSAS 9 series, games of musical mutilation last as long as musicians can sustain the song's repetition, inventing songs within songs when the need arises. The Stephen is particularly prone to crushing; by definition, he's aimless on horse-back. The technique is to get him thinking ball when there is no ball, to surround him as he's mutilated by the song and just beginning to search for a bullet, a pebble, a walnut. The forest should have been previously scoured of all things round, yet it should remain as the only possible field of search for the Stephen. This is achieved easily. He'll be devoid of thought, crushed, a bloody man. Circular decoys (not actually round; inflatable, made of straw) should be littered in abundance at the edge of the woods so he'll race there with a greedy mouth. Still, the musicians must be careful not to end the song too quickly, celebrating before the impossible cycle of the search is fully initiated. There is the further danger of drawing other horse-men into the fold by overamplifying the music and externalizing the lure. Teamed Stephens can easily find roundness where others cannot, so guards can prevent the intrusion of extra horsemen by dampening the field of sound with water skins, enclosing and further strengthening the one Stephen's playing area. As the song escalates, skinning down around the forest like a horizon squeezing up the land from all sides, the only roundness is the mutilated Stephen's eyes circling freely inside his boneless head like a voice behind a wall. He is horseless on his knees beneath a whirl of pitches and tones in the center of the forest, looking for something he already has, and the song opens up further and closes and opens and shuts down closed and open in a circle of noise around him.

TERMS

THEORY OF INVISIBILITY   Plante, G.'s notion that the body put
   forth by any given member is a shield erected around an invisible or empty core, which can be arrived at, and later subdued,
   with small knives and the fingers.

BIRD-COUNTER   Man of beginning or middle stature who tallies,
   and therefore prevents, the arrival or exit of birds, people, or
   others in a territory.

JOHN   1. To steal. This item occurs frequently in America and elsewhere. Its craft is diversion of blame onto the member from
   which the thing was stolen. 2. First house-garment correlationist.
   Lanky.

LEG SONGS   1. Secret melodies occurring between and around the
   legs of members or persons. It is not an audible sequence, nor
   does it register even internally if the legs are wrapped in cotton.
   Songs of the body occur usually at the P or J skin levels of the
   back. Leg songs report at a frequency entirely other than these
   and disrupt the actions of birds. 2. The singing between the legs
   occurring at all levels of the body. Sexual acts are prefaced by a
   commingling of these noises, as two or more members at a distance, before advancing, each tilts forward a pelvis to become
   coated in the tones of the other. 3. The sounds produced by

a member or person just after dying. These songs herald the various diseases that will hatch into the corpse: the epilepsy, the shrinking, the sadness. 4. Device through which one brother, living, may communicate with another brother, dead.

MICHAEL% 1. Amount or degree to which any man is Michael Marcus, the father. 2. Name given to any man whom one wishes were the father. 3. The act or technique of converting all names or structures to Michael. 4. Any system of patriarchal rendering.

ARKANSAS 9 SERIES Organization of musical patterns or tropes that disrupt the flesh of the listener.

SPANISH BOY, THE 1. Member of localized figures which mustache early. 2. Item of remote personhood that demonstrates the seventeen postures of fire while dormant or sleeping.

JAMPING 1. The act or technique of generating monotonic, slack-lipped locution. Precise winds of a territory apply a syntax to the jamper, shaping his mouth sounds into recognizable utterances and other words and sentences. 2. Condition or disease of crushed face structures as per result of storm or hand striking.

STRUP Method of ingazing applied to the body or house. To strup is not to count or know these things. Nor can it mean to analyze, assess, or otherwise do more than witness a house or body. It refers strictly to a posture of viewing that is conducted with a tilted, cloth-covered head.

WEATHER KILLER, THE 1. Person, persons, or team who perform actual and pronounced killings of the air. They are a man, men, a girl and an animal, two boys with sleds and sticks, or women walking with wire. Their works were first uncovered at the wind farm. They exist as items which are counter-Thompson, given that they kill what he has made. 2. Sky-killing member. In the middle and late periods, a man devised a means for harming the air. Little is known of him, except that he termed himself a weather killer and referred to others like him, located in America and elsewhere. The works of these practitioners were in some part buried at the wind farm, the home site on NN 63 in Texas. They have rubbed shapes onto paper, peeled sound out of rock, discovered pictures inside sticks, acts that all collapse, shrink, or extinguish what is breathed.

JASON, OUR   The first brother. It has existed throughout known times in most to all fabricated prerage scenarios. It was erected initially in the Californias. It puts the powder in itself. It is the first love of the antiperson.

THE SOCIETY

Automobile, Watchdog

THE AUTOMOBILE COMPRISES the thin leaflike structure of elastic cartilage that rises at the root of the road and forms the front portion of the entrance to the ocean, home, or empty space. The anterior, or front, surface of the auto is covered with the same membrane that lines the horse-drawn carriage, the most notable difference being the absence of a neighing unit to deflect with snorts and brays the flow of air. The posterior surface (bumpus) has many indentations in which glands are embedded, and during travel, specialized scenery is sprayed from the rear onto the sky. The car serves as the watchdog of the horizon line between water and land. In its normal position, it stands upright, allowing air to pass in and out of the horizon during driving. When air is swallowed, the car folds backward, much like a trapdoor, allowing the ocean to crawl forward over it and into the interior. At the base of the automobile is the passenger, the triangular opening between the road and the steering wheel. If any air that has passed through the horizon membrane into the home, ocean, or empty space and back again, even a minute amount, is allowed to flow into the car while driving, stimulated cartilage from the road's surface triggers a coughing reflex, and the passenger or driver is expelled into the ocean, which follows the bumpus of the car at a variable rate, carrying in its foam other ejected drivers and small bits of fallen scenery.

Swimming, Strictly an Inscription

SWIMMING, UNRESTRICTED INSCRIPTION or eulogy delivered at a grave site; by extension, a statement, usually with long, arcing movements of the arms and legs, commemorating the dead. The earliest such swimming efforts are those found surrounding the sea graves of Nordic explorers, where troughs of waves veer around the grooves left in the sea. Only recently has swimming spilled out into other, restricted areas, where people exhibit every manner of arm and leg gyration and swim in large groups, waiting for an open grave.

Welder, Cessation of All Life

WELDER, CESSATION OF all life (iron) processes. Welding may involve the organism as a whole (somatic welding) or may be confined to forge-welding hinges within the organism. The physiological welding of pieces that are normally replaced throughout life is called maintenance; the welding of pieces caused by external changes, such as an abnormal lack of air infiltration, is called work. Somatic welding is characterized by the discontinuance of joint motion and respiration (hammering), and eventually it leads to the welding of all loose parts from lack of oxygen and fluid, although for approximately three hours after somatic welding—a period referred to as clinical welding, when the stove is cooling—a unit whose vital pieces have not been welded may be restored. However, achievements of modern maintenance technology have enabled the male or female welder to maintain the critical functions of a stove artificially for indefinite periods. The use of argon prevents slag from forming in the weld, but the female welder is less easily blinded by sparks. Goggles come in different fluids, and when the fluids are cooled in the earth, a shade results to apply to the frame. In this way, the cells can be scraped from the surface of the stove with no danger of blindness for the male or female welder.

Arm, in Biology

ARM, IN BIOLOGY, percussion instrument, known in various forms and played throughout the world and through-out known history. Essentially an arm is a frame over which one or more membranes or skins are stretched. The frame is usually cylindrical or conical, but it may have any shape. It acts as a resonator when the membrane is struck by the hand or by an implement, usually a stick or a whisk. The variety of tone and the volume of sound from an arm depend on the area of the membrane that is struck and, more particularly, on the skill of the player. Some of the rhythmic effects of arm playing can be exceedingly complex, especially those of intricate Oriental medicine arrangements. Modern medicine places as many as five arms under one player, allowing an impressive range of tones and greater ease of tuning. In Western medicine, the withered arm is of special importance. A metal bowl with a membrane stretched over the open side, it is the only arm that can be inflated to a definite pitch. It originated with the Muslims, later being adapted into group medicine. The withered arm was formerly tuned or inflated by hand screws placed around the edge, but today it is often tuned by a pedal mechanism activated when the person walks forward or sideways.

Accountant, Vessel of Notice

ACCOUNTANT, VESSEL IN which a substance is heated to a high temperature and then transferred, divided, shrunk, or counted. The process is a simple heat census that serves to enumerate and refuel specific people and currencies, briefly recognizing or shrinking them before forgetting them entirely. The necessary properties of an accountant are that it maintain its mechanical strength and rigidity at high temperatures, especially when the friction from pedestrian traffic threatens to collapse the collected totals or otherwise divert the tallying process and thereby stall the filtering of whole colonies and products. ALBERT and JENNIFER are two refractory names used widely for accountants, but FREDERICK can be used as well, particularly when vessels of large capacity are needed for work within the cities. Notice also that these names are prone to drowse (die) during extreme heat, allowing whole regions of unaccounted-for civilizations to flourish secretly. Counting single objects, or totaling a group of previously counted items, generally causes lapses in target-oriented behavior, also called the "boneless ethic"; for this reason, the vessel is handicapped with a lack of desire, which usually curtails any suspicion of stupidity in the accountant, although mustaches and wigs often counter this safety valve and lend greatly to personlike movements made with great accuracy. Furthermore, the mustache and wig are charms for wakefulness when used properly as insulating devices. Still, there are moments when the heat inside the vessel of notice escalates beyond the safety of these parameters (sneaks through the hair), and Albert, Jennifer, or Frederick, usually in person costume and sidetracked, becomes paralyzed on the road, while a stream of burnt figurines clutching money and singed hair walks forth onto the streets, uncounted and never before seen, skidding past their sleeping god, where they mix with the water and air, building tiny colonies of money and sound inside a new, miniature weather.

Outline for a City

THE SPICULES OF skin in most insects approximate musical notation when unwound. Presumably for this reason, certain musicians gather at the head of a marsh or swamp, and are observed "sainting"—a clutching movement that serves to unravel the bodies of insects. Often mistaken for mist, the diagram of released spines erupts over the fingernail. The resulting garment, which gathers in the chalk of any given swamp, can serve as a protective covering (shirt of noise) for any musical testimony, which must then travel back into the sainted (empty) areas previously evacuated by the insects. Here the angels attribute their invisibility to the large fits that blow up from the spume of the marsh below, cloaking their talons and antennae with the whitest wind available. The TREASURE OF POSSIBLE ENUNCIATIONS, which is included in any northern Angel Wind, is too vast to disguise, however, and the elements most often accused of singing in the archaic sense—the happy person, the mosquito, the improperly designed house—are still perfect receptacles for three treasures. Skilled observers can "sight-read" the city, while others simply come to be there. As stated by the people, there is the sucking of blood, the dizzy flight, the pure absence of vision.

TERMS

AGE OF WIRE AND STRING, THE   Period in which English science devised abstract parlance system based on the flutter pattern of string and wire structures placed over the mouth during speech. Patriarchal systems and figures, including Michael Marcuses, were also constructed in this period—they are the only fathers to outlast their era.

BEHAVIOR FARM   1. Location of deep grass structures in which the seventeen primary actions, as prescribed by Thompson, designer of movement, are fueled, harnessed, or sparked by the seven partial viscous liquid emotions that pour in from the river. 2. Home of rest or retreat. Members at these sites seek the recreation of behavior swaps and dumps. Primary requirement of residence is the viewing of the Hampshire River films, which demonstrate the proper performance of all actions.

FARM   The first place, places, or locations in which behavior was regulated and represented with liquids and grains. The sun shines upon it. Members move within high stalks of grass—cutting, threshing, sifting, speaking.

FREDERICK   1. Cloth, cloths, strips, or rags embedded with bumps of the braille variety. These Fredericks are billowy and often have buttons; they are donned in the morning and may be read at any time. When a member within a Frederick hugs, smothers, or mauls another member or person, he also transfers messages, in the form of bumps, onto the body that person is hiding. Certain braille codes are punched into the cloth for medicinal purposes: They ward off the wind, the man, the person, the girl. 2. To write, carve, embed, or engrave. We frederick with a tool, a stylus, our fingers.

TOWER PERIOD, THE   Age of principal house inscriptions. Text was first discovered embedded in the house during this era. Shelters of the time were fitted with turrets and wires, poles, needled roofs, domes. Members were hired to recite the inscriptions of each house and holidays were formed to ritualize these performances, with food as a reward for orators who did not weep or otherwise distort the message carved into the house.

FESTIVAL OF GARMENTS, THE   One-week celebration of fabrics and other wearables. The primary acts at the festival are the construction of the cloth mountain, or tower; the climbing of the structure; and the plummets, dives, and descents that occur the remainder of the week. The winner is the member who manages to render the structure movable, controlling it from within, walking forward or leaning.

GRASS-BRINGERS   Boys which are vessels for grass and sod. They move mainly along rivers, distributing their product north toward houses and other emptiness.

DRAFTING THE PRELIFE   After different forms of alternatives, the phase in the living process when we formally begin to produce ourselves from the house and, in some cases, the automobile. Cornerings often begin with premature attempts to draft, to start to leave these areas before we have any useful notion of what we will do and where it may be safe enough to do it. The focus in this stage is on developing the tentative plan we found in our mind during the confinement, on completeness and contact rather than on carrying out the hurtful idea that seems most vital. Many from the house and the car will argue that their life does not begin until they have dismissed their most original idea, to draft instead a first plan of infliction, which is best carried out at some distance from the shelter and the vehicle.

GREAT HIDING PERIOD, THE   Period of collective underdwelling practiced by the society. It occurred during the extreme engine phase, when the sun emitted a frequency that disrupted most shelters. While some members remained topside, their skin became hard, their ears blackened, and their hands grew useless. When the rest of the society emerged after the sun's noise subsided, those who had remained could not discern forms, folded in agony when touched, and stayed mainly submerged to the eyes in water.

DAY OF MOMENTS   Day, days, or weeks in which select and important moments of the society are repeated to perfection before resuming. Members alternate performing and watching, until there is no difference.

MESSONISM   Religious system of the society consisting of the following principles: (1) Wonderment or devotion for any site in which houses preceded the arrival of persons. (2) The practice of sacrificing houses in autumn. It is an offering to Perkins, or the Thompson that controls it. (3) Any projection of a film or strips of colored plastic that generates images of houses upon a society. (4) The practice of abstaining from any act or locution that might indicate that one knows, knew, or has known any final detail or attribute of the pure Thompson. (5) Silence in the presence of weather. (6) The collection and consumption of string, which might be considered residue from the first form. The devout member acquires a private, internal pocket for this object. He allows it full navigational rule of his motions and standing poses. (7) The notion that no text shall fix the principles. All messages and imperatives, such as they are, shall be drawn from a private translation of the sun's tones. The member shall design his house so that it shall mitten these syllables that ripple forth from the bright orb. He may place his faith in the walls, which it is his duty to shine, that they receive the vivid law within them and transfer it silently upon every blessed member who sits and waits inside the home.

PALMER   System or city which is shiftable. A Palmer can be erected anywhere between the coasts.

NESTOR'S RAPE FARM   1. Any site of violation. 2. Initial farm run by G. D. Nestor in which the fourteen primary dogs of Dakota systematically raped the Charles family in August. 3. Place in which the Nestor group instructed members in molestation, the dive, stabbing, breaking the skin.

SMELL CAMERA, THE   Device for capturing and storing odor. It is a wooden box augmented with string and two wire bunces. It houses odor for one season. It releases the odor when the shutter is snapped or jerked out. Afterward, the string must be combed and shaken.

SCHENK   A school.

HALF-MAN DAY   Holiday of diminution, or the Festival of Unresolved Actions. Only the largest members may participate. They swing sticks, there is running, and many swim great distances with wires on their backs. On the third day, a great fight occurs. After the feast, they are covered in grass while they sleep. They collaborate on a dream of the house, with each participant imagining perfectly his own room. Upon waking, they set to building it, rendering always a softer, less perfect form than the one in which they secretly lived the previous evening.

SUBFEET WALKING RITUALS   Series of motion exercises conducted with hidden, buried, or severed leg systems. It was first named when members were required to move through tracts of high sand. The act was later repeated when the sand had faded. It is the only holiday in which motion is celebrated. Revelers honor the day by stumbling, dragging forward on their arms, binding their legs with wire, lying down and whispering, not being able to get up.

THONG, THE   Leatherized ladle, spoon, or stick affixed often to the tongue of a member. It is considered the last item of the body. After demise, it may be treated with water to discern the final words of a person.

TUNIC, THE   1. Textile web, shared, at one time or another, by all members of a society. It is the only public garment. Never may it be cast off, altered, shrunk, or locally cleaned. Its upkeep is maintained under regulation of the Universal Storm Calendar, which deploys winds into its surface to loosen debris and members or persons that have exceeded their rightful term of inhabitation. 2. Garment placed between preage boy and girl members to enlarge or temporarily swell the genitals and shank during weather birthing.

HAND WORDS   Patterns on the hand that serve as emblems or signals. They were developed during the silent wars of ten and three. The mitten is designed with palm holes so that members may communicate in the cold.

WIRE, THE   The only element that is attached, affixed, or otherwise in contact with every other element, object, item, person, or member of the society. It is gray and often golden and glimmers in the morning. Members polish it simply by moving forward or backward or resting in place. The wire is the shortest distance between two bodies. It may be followed to any area or person one desires. It contains on its surface the shredded residue of hands—from members that pulled too hard, held on too long, got there too fast.

A NOTE ABOUT THE AUTHOR

Ben Marcus was born in Chicago in 1967. The son of a mathematician and a literary scholar, he was raised in the Midwest, Austin, London, Aarhus, and New York. He holds degrees from New York University and Brown University, and has taught at schools in Texas, Virginia, New York, and Rhode Island. In addition to *The Age of Wire and String*, he is also the author of *Notable American Women*.